Praise for Stephen Mitchell's *Gilgamesh*

"Stephen Mitchell's *Gilgamesh* is a wonderful version. It is as eloquent and nuanced as his translations of Rilke. This is certainly the best that I have seen in English." —Harold Bloom

"Reading Stephen Mitchell's marvelously clear and vivid rendering makes me feel that I am encountering *Gilgamesh* for the first time." —Elaine Pagels, author of *The Gnostic Gospels*

"Ingenious and very readable." —*The New York Review of Books*

"It was a revelation. The translation is superb." —Harold Pinter

"A magnificent new rendering. . . . Propels the reader along through the subtle, muscular music of its rhythms. The language is spare, sinuous, pellucid and often striking. For the reader who wishes to breathe in the spirit of this epic, to relate to it as a work of literature rather than to interpret it as a series of fragments recording some distant legend, Mitchell produces what should become recognized as the standard text. Read it and sense all the wisdom and complexity of the original. . . ." —*The Times* (London)

"A very readable version in stately verse. . . . Warmly recommended. . . . Retains just enough of the strangeness of the original and its robust imagery to capture its essence, and by smoothing the fragments into a coherent narrative he highlights the work's essential themes." —*The Washington Post*

"Here is the wisdom and lyrical beauty of yore rendered, offered us anew, by a distinguished, ever-so-knowing translator and poet who has given so many of us a wondrous education these past years. Mitchell connects us to treasures of the past brought alive by his broad and deep sensibility."
—Robert Coles, James Agee Professor of Social Ethics, Harvard University

"Stephen Mitchell's fresh new rendition of mankind's oldest recorded myth is quite wonderful in its limpidity and the immediacy of its live emotions."
—Peter Matthiessen, author of *At Play in the Fields of the Lord*

"As fast-paced and thrilling as a contemporary action film. . . . This wonderful new version of the story of Gilgamesh shows how the story came to achieve literary immortality—not because it is a rare ancient artifact, but because reading it can make people in the here and now feel more completely alive."
—*Publishers Weekly* (starred review)

"Since its discovery, the 3,500-year-old Mesopotamian saga has been rendered into English countless times. Not until now, however, has it found a translation capable of evoking its great power—a translation vigorous in its narration, translucent in its poetry and incisive in its depiction of our clever, struggling, frail humanity. Stephen Mitchell's *Gilgamesh* is a masterpiece of storytelling, or re-telling."
—*Archaeology Odyssey*

"A powerful translation of an eerie and unsettling ancient epic. . . . The most pellucid version of the epic yet to have been written in English, but . . . most startling and admirable . . . is the fact that Mitchell has not sacrificed a sense of the weird on the altar of readability."
—*The Daily Telegraph* (London)

"As narrative verse, this *Gilgamesh* gently entrances and enthralls. Its liquid, intimate four-stressed lines . . . negotiate the rapid shifts between everyday pleasures, heroic feats, and blazing visions in this mythic world where the sensual and spiritual always intersect. Mitchell manages to slip the mesmerizing incantations of the verse . . . into his reader's bloodstream."
—*The Independent* (London)

"Remarkable: a rendition that, while taking no great liberties with the text, somehow makes it available as a work of literature, rather than as a set of fragments from a vanished cosmology. . . . The lines of verse move swiftly, gracefully . . . the diction is simple and clean, evoking the sense of a time when the world was new and first being named. Reading this *Gilgamesh* gave me a sense, for the first time, of understanding Rilke's devotion to the poem."
—*Newsday*

"Henceforth, no person can consider himself . . . fully educated without having read, in addition to the Bible, Homer, and Shakespeare, this oddly humane and curiously modern story."
—*Sun-Sentinel* (Ft. Lauderdale)

"Mitchell, the noted translator of many of the world's seminal spiritual texts, has reached back to ancient Mesopotamia to bring out a version of . . . literature's first hero story that speaks to modern times."
—*San Francisco Chronicle*

"Mitchell's version of *Gilgamesh* . . . clips along like an action novel. With its contemporary language and modernized narrative, it would find enthusiastic readers even among those who have no interest in classic literature."
—*City Paper* (Baltimore)

BY STEPHEN MITCHELL

POETRY

Parables and Portraits

FICTION

The Frog Prince

Meetings with the Archangel

NONFICTION

Loving What Is: Four Questions that Can Change Your Life
(with Byron Katie)

The Gospel According to Jesus

TRANSLATIONS AND ADAPTATIONS

Gilgamesh

Bhagavad Gita

Real Power: Business Lessons from the Tao Te Ching
(with James A. Autry)

Full Woman, Fleshly Apple, Hot Moon:
Selected Poems of Pablo Neruda

GILGAMESH

A New English Version

STEPHEN MITCHELL

ATRIA PAPERBACK

New York ◆ London ◆ Toronto ◆ Sydney ◆ New Delhi

ATRIA PAPERBACK
A Division of Simon & Schuster, Inc.
1230 Avenue of the Americas
New York, NY 10020

First Atria Paperback edition September 2013

ATRIA PAPERBACK and colophon are trademarks
of Simon & Schuster, Inc.

For information about special discounts for bulk purchases,
please contact Simon & Schuster Special Sales:
1-866-506-1949 or business@simonandschuster.com.

The Simon & Schuster Speakers Bureau can bring authors to your
live event. For more information or to book an event, contact the
Simon & Schuster Speakers Bureau at 1-866-248-3049 or visit our
website at www.simonspeakers.com.

Design by Joel Avirom and Jason Snyder
Illustrations by Jason Snyder

Manufactured in the United States of America

20   19   18

The Library of Congress has cataloged the Free Press hardcover edition as follows:
Gilgamesh. English.
  Gilgamesh / a new English version [by] Stephen Mitchell.
    p. cm.
Includes bibliographical references.
1. Epic poetry, Assyro-Babylonian—Translations into English.
I. Mitchell, Stephen, 1943– II. Title.
  PJ3771.5.G5E5 2004
  892′.1—dc22
  2004050072

ISBN 978-0-7432-6164-7
ISBN 978-0-7432-6169-2 (pbk)
ISBN 978-1-4391-0474-3 (ebook)

To Katie

CONTENTS

INTRODUCTION

THE OLDEST STORY
IN THE WORLD

In Iraq, when the dust blows, stopping men and tanks, it brings with it memories of an ancient world, much older than Islam or Christianity. Western civilization originated from that place between the Tigris and the Euphrates, where Hammurabi created his legal code and where *Gilgamesh* was written—the oldest story in the world, a thousand years older than the *Iliad* or the Bible. Its hero was a historical king who reigned in the Mesopotamian city of Uruk in about 2750 BCE. In the epic, he has an intimate friend, Enkidu, a naked wild man who has been civilized through the erotic arts of a temple priestess. With him Gilgamesh battles monsters, and when Enkidu dies, he is inconsolable. He sets out on a desperate journey to find the one man who can tell him how to escape death.

Part of the fascination of *Gilgamesh* is that, like any great work of literature, it has much to tell us about ourselves. In giving voice to grief and the fear of death, perhaps more powerfully than any book written after it, in portraying love and vulnerability and the quest for wisdom, it has become a personal testimony for millions of readers in dozens of languages. But it also has a particular relevance in today's world, with its polarized fundamentalisms, each side fervently believing in its own righteousness, each on a crusade, or jihad, against what it perceives as an evil enemy. The hero of this epic is an antihero, a superman (a superpower, one might say) who doesn't know the difference between strength and arrogance. By preemptively attacking a monster, he brings on himself a disaster that can only be overcome by an agonizing journey, a quest that results in wisdom by proving its own futility. The epic has an extraordinarily sophisticated moral intelligence. In its emphasis on balance and in its refusal to side with either hero or monster, it leads us to question our dangerous certainties about good and evil.

I began this version of *Gilgamesh* because I had never been convinced by the language of any translation of it that I'd read. I wanted to find a genuine voice for the poem: words that were lithe and muscular enough to match the power of the story. If I have succeeded, readers will discover that, rather than standing before an antiquity in a glass case, they have entered a literary masterpiece that is as startlingly alive today as it was three and a half millennia ago.

ORIGINS

Gilgamesh is a work that in the intensity of its imagination stands beside the great stories of Homer and the Bible. Yet for two thousand years, all traces of it were lost. The baked clay tablets on which it was inscribed in cuneiform characters lay buried in the rubble of cities across the ancient Near East, waiting for people from another world to read them. It wasn't until 1850 that the first fragments were discovered among the ruins of Nineveh, and the text wasn't deciphered and translated for several decades afterward. The great poet Rainer Maria Rilke may have been the first reader discerning enough to recognize its true literary stature. *"Gilgamesh* is stupendous!" he wrote at the end of 1916. "I . . . consider it to be among the greatest things that can happen to a person." "I have immersed myself in [it], and in these truly gigantic fragments I have experienced measures and forms that belong with the supreme works that the conjuring Word has ever produced." In Rilke's consciousness, *Gilgamesh,* like a magnificent Aladdin's palace that has instantly materialized out of nowhere, makes its first appearance as a masterpiece of world literature.

The story of its discovery and decipherment is itself as fabulous as a tale from *The Thousand and One Nights.* A young English traveler named Austen Henry Layard, who was passing through the Middle East on his way to Ceylon, heard that there were antiquities buried in the mounds of what is now the city of Mosul, halted his journey, and began excavations in 1844. These mounds turned out to contain the ruined palaces of Nineveh, the ancient capital of Assyria, including what was left of the library of the last great Assyrian king, Ashurbanipal (668–627 BCE). "In amazement" Layard and his assistant Hormuzd Rassam "found room after room lined with carved stone bas-reliefs of demons and deities, scenes of battle, royal hunts and ceremonies; doorways flanked by enormous winged bulls and lions; and, inside some of the chambers, tens of thousands of clay tablets inscribed with the curious, and then undeciphered, cuneiform ('wedge-shaped') script." Over twenty-five thousand of these tablets were shipped back to the British Museum.

When cuneiform was officially deciphered in 1857, scholars discovered that the tablets were written in Akkadian, an ancient Semitic language cognate with Hebrew and Arabic. Fifteen years went by before anyone noticed the tablets on which *Gilgamesh* was inscribed. Then, in 1872, a young British Museum curator named George Smith realized that one of the fragments told the story of a Babylonian Noah, who survived a great flood sent by the gods. "On looking down the third column," Smith wrote, "my eye caught the statement that the ship rested on the mountains of Nizir, followed by the account of the sending forth of the dove, and its finding no resting-place and returning. I saw at once that I had here discovered a portion at least of the Chaldean account of the Deluge." To a Victorian this was a spectacular discovery, because it seemed to be independent corroboration of the historicity of the biblical Flood (Victorians believed that the Genesis story was much older than it is). When Smith saw these lines, according to a later account, he said, " 'I am the first man to read that after more than two thousand years of oblivion!' Setting the tablet on the table," the account continues, "he jumped up and rushed about the room in a great state of excitement, and, to the astonishment of those present, began to undress himself." We aren't told if he took off just his coat or if he continued to strip down further. I like to imagine him in his euphoria going all the way and running stark naked, like Enkidu, among the astonished black-clad Victorian scholars.

Smith's announcement, made on December 3, 1872 to the newly formed Society of Biblical Archaeology, that he had discovered an account of the Flood on one of the Assyrian tablets caused a major stir, and soon more fragments of *Gilgamesh* were unearthed at Nineveh and in the ruins of other ancient cities. His translation of the fragments that had been discovered up to then was published in 1876. Though to a modern reader it seems quaint and almost surrealistic in its many mistaken guesses, and is often fragmentary to the point of incoherence, it was an important pioneering effort.

Today, more than a century and a quarter later, many more fragments have surfaced, the language is much better understood, and scholars can trace the history of the text with some degree of confidence. Briefly, here is the consensus.

Legends about Gilgamesh probably began to arise shortly after the death of the historical king. The earliest texts that have survived, which date from about 2100 BCE, are five separate and independent poems in Sumerian, entitled "Gilgamesh and Aga," "Gilgamesh and Huwawa," "Gilgamesh and the Bull of Heaven," "Gilgamesh and the Underworld," and "The Death of Gilgamesh." (Sumerian is a non-Semitic language unrelated to any other that we know, and is as distant from Akkadian as Chinese is from English. It became the learned language of ancient Mesopotamia and was part of the scribal curriculum.) These five poems—written in a leisurely, repetitive, hieratic style, much less condensed and vivid than the Akkadian epic—would have been familiar to later poets and editors.

The direct ancestor of the eleven clay tablets dug up at Nineveh is called the Old Babylonian version. It was written in Akkadian (of which Babylonian is a dialect) and dates from about 1700 BCE; eleven fragments have survived, including three tablets that are almost complete. This version, though it paraphrases a few episodes in the Sumerian *Gilgamesh* texts, is an original poem, the first *Epic of Gilgamesh*. In its themes and its form, it is essentially the same poem as its Ninevite descendent: a story about friendship, the death of the beloved, and the quest for immortality.

Some five hundred years after the Old Babylonian version was written, a scholar-priest named Sîn-lēqi-unninni revised and elaborated on it. His epic, which scholars call the Standard Version, is the basis for all modern translations. As of now, with seventy-three fragments discovered, slightly fewer than two thousand of the three thousand lines of the original text exist in readable, continuous form; the rest is damaged or missing, and there are many gaps in the sections that have survived.

We don't know exactly what Sîn-lēqi-unninni's contribution to the Standard Version was, since so few fragments of the Old Babylonian version have survived for comparison. From what we can see, he is often a conservative editor, following the older version line for line, with few if any changes in vocabulary and word order. Sometimes, though, he expands or contracts, drops passages or adds them, and functions not as

an editor but as an original poet. The two major passages that we know
he added, the Prologue and the priestess Shamhat's speech inviting
Enkidu to Uruk, have the vividness and density of great art.

The *Gilgamesh* that you are about to read is a sometimes free,
sometimes close adaptation into English verse of Sîn-lēqi-unninni's
Standard Version.* Even scholars making literal translations don't
simply translate the Standard Version; they fill in some of the textual
gaps with passages from other versions, the Old Babylonian being
the most important. I have taken this practice further: occasionally,
when the Standard Version is particularly fragmentary, I have sup-
plemented it with passages from the Sumerian *Gilgamesh* poems. I
have also added lines or short passages to bridge the gaps or to clar-
ify the story. My intention throughout has been to re-create the
ancient epic, as a contemporary poem, in the parallel universe of the
English language.

CIVILIZING THE WILD MAN

G*ilgamesh* is the story of a hero's journey; one might say that it is
the mother of all heroes' journeys, with its huge uninhibited
mythic presences moving through a landscape of dream. It is also the
story of how a man becomes civilized, how he learns to rule himself
and therefore his people, and to act with temperance, wisdom, and
piety. The poem begins with the city and ends with it.

---

* See "About This Version," p. 65.

In the first lines of his Prologue, Sîn-lēqi-unninni states the breadth and depth of what his hero had endured: "He had seen everything, had experienced all emotions." The next seven lines tell us the essential details, not even bothering to mention the hero's name. Gilgamesh had traveled to the edge of the world and been granted knowledge of the primeval days of humanity; he had survived the journey and returned to restore the great temple of Ishtar and Uruk's then famous six-mile-long wall.

And now, after this summary, something fascinating happens. Sîn-lēqi-unninni turns to his readers and invites them to survey the great city for themselves:

> See how its ramparts gleam like copper in the sun.
> Climb the stone staircase, more ancient than the mind
>   can imagine,
> approach the Eanna Temple, sacred to Ishtar,
> a temple that no king has equaled in size or beauty,
> walk on the wall of Uruk, follow its course
> around the city, inspect its mighty foundations,
> examine its brickwork, how masterfully it is built,
> observe the land it encloses: the palm trees, the gardens,
> the orchards, the glorious palaces and temples, the shops
> and marketplaces, the houses, the public squares.

It is a very strange and touching moment. The poet is ostensibly addressing an audience of ancient Babylonians in 1200 BCE, directing

them to admire a city that was built in time immemorial. But the readers, as it turns out, are you and I. We are the ones who are being invited, more than three thousand years later, to walk on the wall of Uruk and observe the splendor and bustling life of the great city. The invitation is touching not because the city is in ruins and the civilization has been destroyed—this is not an ironic "Ozymandias" moment—but because in our imagination we *can* climb the ancient stone staircase and observe the lush gardens and orchards, the palaces and temples, the shops and marketplaces, the houses, the public squares, and share the poet's amazement and pride in his city.

Then Sîn-lēqi-unninni's invitation becomes more intimate. "Find the cornerstone," he tells us,

> and under it the copper box
> that is marked with his name. Unlock it. Open the lid.
> Take out the tablet of lapis lazuli. Read
> how Gilgamesh suffered all and accomplished all.

I doubt whether even in 1200 BCE this was meant to be taken literally. Even to an ancient Babylonian reader, the lines would have been vivid enough to make the physical act unnecessary. As we read the instructions, we can see ourselves finding the cornerstone, taking out the copper box, unlocking it, opening its lid, and taking out the priceless tablet of lapis lazuli, which turns out, in the end, to be the very poem we are about to read. We are looking beneath the surface of things, into the hidden places, the locked repositories of human experience. The trials that Gilgamesh himself is supposed to have written down long ago are now being revealed to us in words that, whether "carved on stone tablets" or printed on paper, create their own sense of authenticity. They issue directly from the source: if not from the historical Gilgamesh, then from a poet who has imagined that hero's experience intensely enough for it to be true.

The Old Babylonian poem that Sîn-lēqi-unninni inherited begins with the phrase "Surpassing all kings." It describes Gilgamesh as a gigantic and manic young man (his name may mean "The Old Man is a Young Man"), a warrior, and, after his return, as a good king and benefactor to his people: a combination of Goliath and David. But to begin with he is a tyrant. When we first enter the poem, there is an essential imbalance in the city; something has gone drastically wrong. The man of unsurpassable courage and inexhaustible energy has become a monster of selfishness; the shepherd has become a wolf. He oppresses the young men, perhaps with forced labor, and oppresses the young women, perhaps with his ravenous sexual appetite. Because he is an absolute monarch (and two-thirds divine into the bargain), no one dares to criticize him. The people call out to heaven, like the Israelite slaves in Exodus, and their cry is heard. But Anu, father of the gods, doesn't intervene directly. He sends help in a deliciously roundabout way. He asks the great mother goddess, Aruru, to reenact her first creation of human beings:

"Now go and create
a double for Gilgamesh, his second self,

a man who equals his strength and courage,
a man who equals his stormy heart.
Create a new hero, let them balance each other
perfectly, so that Uruk has peace."

Like the Lord God in Genesis, Aruru forms a man from the dust of the ground, and he becomes a living being, the original man himself: natural, innocent, solitary. This second Adam will find "a help meet for him" not in a woman but in the man for whose sake he was created. Thus begins—a thousand years before Achilles and Patroclus, or David and Jonathan—the first great friendship in literature.

Enkidu is indeed Gilgamesh's double, so huge and powerful that when people see him they are struck with awe. But he is also Gilgamesh's opposite and mirror image: two-thirds animal to Gilgamesh's two-thirds divine. These animal qualities are actually much more attractive than the divine ones. Where Gilgamesh is arrogant, Enkidu is childlike; where Gilgamesh is violent, Enkidu is peaceful, a naked herbivore among the herds. He lives and wanders with them from pasture to pasture, and (as we learn later in the poem) he drives away marauding predators, thus acting as both sheep and shepherd. With his natural altruism, he is also the original animal activist, setting his friends free from human pits and traps.

When the trapper discovers Enkidu drinking with the animals at a waterhole, he is filled with dread, as if he has seen a bigfoot or abominable snowman. What makes his face go white and his legs shake is not the fear of being harmed by a powerful savage (after all, he doesn't

have to get any closer): it is the fear of being face to face with primor-
dial humanity, the thing itself. He goes to his father for advice, and the
father sends him on to Gilgamesh, who "will know what to do."

Gilgamesh may be a tyrant, but he is an insightful one. He does
know what to do about the wild man, and he tells it to the trapper
without a moment's hesitation. "Go to the temple of Ishtar," he says,

> "ask them there for a woman named Shamhat,
> one of the priestesses who give their bodies
> to any man, in honor of the goddess.
> Take her into the wilderness.
> When the animals are drinking at the waterhole,
> tell her to strip off her robe and lie there
> naked, ready, with her legs apart.
> The wild man will approach. Let her use her love-arts.
> Nature will take its course, and then
> the animals who knew him in the wilderness
> will be bewildered, and will leave him forever."

It is a startling recommendation, especially coming from a man whose
modus operandi is force. We might have expected him to send out a
battalion to hunt down and capture Enkidu. Instead, he commissions
a single woman. Somehow he knows that Enkidu needs to be tamed
rather than captured, and that the only way to civilize him is through
the power of eros. He doesn't seem to suspect, however, that the wild
man has been sent by the gods to civilize *him*.

The poem says nothing about Gilgamesh's relationship to Shamhat. Does he know how skilled she is because he has made love with her himself at the temple? Is he a regular client? Or has he just heard of her prowess? All we are told is that he knows she is the right woman for the job.

Shamhat is one of the most fascinating characters in *Gilgamesh*. If we want to appreciate her role as an ancient Babylonian cultic prostitute, our imagination needs to bypass any filters of romantic love, Judeo-Christian morality, male lubricity, or female indignation. Actually, we have no word in English for what Shamhat is. The Akkadian words *harīmtu* and *šamḫātu* certainly do not mean "prostitute" in our sense of the term, a woman who sells herself for personal gain. She is a priestess of Ishtar, the goddess of love, and, as a kind of reverse nun, has dedicated her life to what the Babylonians considered the sacred mystery of sexual union. In opening to the anonymous man who appears before her in the temple, young or old, handsome or ugly, she is opening to Everyman—that is, to God. She has become an incarnation of the goddess, and with her own body reenacts the cosmic marriage. As a pure servant of eros, she is a vessel for the force that moves the stars, the force that through the green fuse drives the flower.

In a passage about the attractions of Uruk that was added in the Standard Version, Sîn-lēqi-unninni mentions Ishtar's priestesses with enormous pride:

"Come," said Shamhat, "let us go to Uruk,
I will lead you to Gilgamesh the mighty king.

You will see the great city with its massive wall,
you will see the young men dressed in their splendor,
in the finest linen and embroidered wool,
brilliantly colored, with fringed shawls and wide belts.
Every day is a festival in Uruk,
with people singing and dancing in the streets,
musicians playing their lyres and drums,
the lovely priestesses standing before
the temple of Ishtar, chatting and laughing,
flushed with sexual joy, and ready
to serve men's pleasure, in honor of the goddess,
so that even old men are aroused from their beds."

How the poet loves his city! The great wall, the colors, the finery, the music and dancing—they all form the texture of the continuous celebration of life that makes this passage so alive. Part of the enjoyment he conveys is that in Uruk male sexual desire is so abundantly gratified. But it is the lovely, joyful priestesses, themselves gratified in the act of gratification, who light up his portrait of the city. Their laughter and sexual glow is for him one of the principal glories of civilization.

The trapper finds Shamhat and tells her of the king's command. Shamhat has been trained in the art of surrender, and I imagine her as giving her full consent to the mission, dangerous though it might be. The creature she will be offering herself to is, after all, an unknown. He may be ferocious, he may be more beast than man, he may even tear her to shreds, for all she knows (and she probably

knows that the very sight of him filled the trapper with dread). But she agrees to go—calmly, as I imagine her, trusting in her art and in the power of eros.

The waterhole is a three days' hike through the wilderness, and the poet could easily have inserted dialogues here between the young priestess of Ishtar and the trapper. What was she feeling on the long and perhaps physically taxing walk? Was she afraid? What did she ask him about his life, about Enkidu? Was he dazzled by her sexual presence? Was he tempted? Did they make love, or was that forbidden? What did he ask her, and what did she answer, about the life of the city, about her experiences in the temple, about Gilgamesh the king? The poet compresses all the dramatic possibilities of these three days into two lines:

> For three days they walked. On the third day
> they reached the waterhole. There they waited.

The economy of his art is exquisite.

For another two days Shamhat and the trapper wait at the waterhole. When Enkidu appears, Shamhat follows directions (not that a skilled priestess of Ishtar would have needed directions), and events unfold just as Gilgamesh predicted they would. It is a deeply moving episode, especially if we have in the back of our minds the Genesis myth of the loss of human innocence. Here Shamhat plays the role of Eve, but she is a benign seductress, leading Enkidu not into the knowledge of a polarized good and evil, but into the glories of sexuality, the intimate understanding of what a woman is, and

self-awareness as a human being. There is no serpent in this garden, no anxious deity announcing prohibitions and punishments. Again, the poet's economy is superb. The seven days of lovemaking are described in the simplest of terms; compressed into seven lines is a whole epic of sexual initiation. Enkidu, in his innocence and trust, follows where his penis points, and discovers in himself an elemental potency, a state of perpetual erection. For Shamhat's part, however frightened she may be as the enormous hairy creature approaches, she takes him in lovingly, and keeps taking him in for seven days—a feat that is at least equal to any of the showier male heroics later in the poem.

> She used her love-arts, she took his breath
> with her kisses, held nothing back, and showed him
> what a woman is. For seven days
> he stayed erect and made love with her.

There are no traces of puritan consciousness in the culture of this poem: sex is seen as a civilizing event rather than as something dangerous to the social order. One would be interested to know precisely what the love-arts of a Babylonian priestess were, but this also the poet leaves to the imagination. Whatever the graphic details, Shamhat obviously does her job well. Adept and lavishly generous, she totally justifies Gilgamesh's confidence in her.

At the end of seven days, when he has had enough of the nonstop lovemaking, Enkidu tries to rejoin his animals, but they dart away

at full speed, like the fawn that emerges with Alice from the wood where things have no names. Enkidu no longer has the unconscious mind of an animal or the vital force he had as a child of the wilderness. Something has been lost, but it is not paradise. In fact, Enkidu is about to enter another kind of paradise: civilization, the city where every day is a festival. Walking back to Shamhat, he realizes that although he can no longer run like an animal, he has gained something that more than makes up for his lost powers. In knowing Shamhat sexually, his mind has been enlarged: he has begun to know himself. He sits down at her feet, and as he listens he discovers that he can understand human language. He also discovers for himself what the Lord God realizes for Adam in Genesis, that "it is not good that the man should be alone." In this longing for a true friend, he intuits what he was created for.

Shamhat not only initiates Enkidu into self-awareness between her civilizing thighs; she invites him to Uruk, gives him human clothing, and teaches him to eat human food in the hut of some shepherds who live conveniently nearby. She acts as a patient, loving mother as she guides him through this rite of passage. The scene at the shepherds' table is both hilarious and touching, with its shame-free awareness that initiation into humanity means knowing what it is to be sexual, intoxicated, and clean.

> They led him to their table, they put bread and beer
> in front of him. Enkidu sat and stared,
> he had never seen human food, he didn't
> know what to do. Then Shamhat said,

"Go ahead, Enkidu. This is food,
we humans eat and drink this." Warily
he tasted the bread. Then he ate a piece,
he ate a whole loaf, then ate another,
he ate until he was full, drank seven
pitchers of the beer, his heart grew light,
his face glowed, and he sang out with joy.
He had his hair cut, he washed, he rubbed
sweet oil into his skin, and became
fully human.

We get three further glimpses of Shamhat: as she and Enkidu
make love yet again, as she humbly carries out a request of his, and
finally, as she accompanies him to Uruk. Then, having completed her
mission, she is gone.

THE CHALLENGE

Great-walled Uruk, city of gardens and temples and public
squares, is the paradise of Shamhat's description, but it is also
a place of suffering, where the people cry out because of Gilgamesh's
tyranny. The two realities coexist; they appear according to one's
perception, the way light is either particle or wave; it all depends on
how one approaches the city. When she invites Enkidu to Uruk,
Shamhat suggests that he approach with the eyes of appreciation,
that he stand before Gilgamesh and "gaze with wonder" at his mag-

nificence. But Enkidu isn't ready for this. He needs to approach him as a tyrant and an adversary.

Shamhat did in fact introduce Gilgamesh as a tyrant the first time she mentioned him, without a hint of the panegyric that is to follow:

> "Let me take you
> to great-walled Uruk, to the temple of Ishtar,
> to the palace of Gilgamesh the mighty king,
> who in his arrogance oppresses the people,
> trampling upon them like a wild bull."

Enkidu's response is surprising. He doesn't bristle or become white with anger, as he does later when he hears of Gilgamesh's apparent right to sleep with any about-to-be-married virgin. He intuits something in Gilgamesh beyond his brute strength and callousness. His longing is a recognition that floats up toward the surface of his consciousness, a recognition, before the fact, that however unjust Gilgamesh may be, they are meant for each other.

> Deep in his heart he felt something stir,
> a longing he had never known before,
> the longing for a true friend.

But immediately he shifts from this poignant, introspective silence to an aggressive stance that matches Gilgamesh in arrogance. "I will challenge him," Enkidu says.

"I will shout to his face:
'I am the mightiest! *I* am the man
who can make the world tremble! *I* am supreme!' "

If a strong young gorilla had the power of speech, this is what he
might cry out to the alpha male with his harem of wives. The chal-
lenge is touching in its primitiveness. There is no Homeric subtlety or
eloquence here, just testosterone speaking. *Another hero? I will fight him!*
Enkidu needs to test himself, to enter civilization with a chip on his
shoulder the size of a cedar trunk. Shamhat, speaking as his teacher,
suggests that he approach Gilgamesh from a different perspective:

"I will show you Gilgamesh the mighty king,
the hero destined for both joy and grief.
You will stand before him and gaze with wonder,
you will see how handsome, how virile he is,
how his body pulses with erotic power.
He is even taller and stronger than you—
so full of life-force that he needs no sleep.
Enkidu, put aside your aggression."

But Enkidu is having none of it. Nothing can bring him out of his male
challenge mode.

The specific impetus for the trip to Uruk comes from the
mouth of a young man who passes Enkidu and Shamhat, as they are
making love again, on his way to Uruk for a wedding that he has

catered. Enkidu's curiosity is aroused more highly than his passion; he interrupts the coitus and sends Shamhat over to make inquiries. The young man describes what will happen at the end of the ceremony:

> "The priest will bless the young couple, the guests
> will rejoice, the bridegroom will step aside,
> and the virgin will wait in the marriage bed
> for Gilgamesh, king of great-walled Uruk.
> It is he who mates first with the lawful wife.
> After he is done, the bridegroom follows.
> This is the order that the gods have decreed.
> From the moment the king's birth-cord was cut,
> every girl's hymen has belonged to him."

"As he listened," we are told, "Enkidu's face went pale / with anger," but we aren't told why he is angry. Is this the indiscriminate fury of a young challenger? Is he feeling moral outrage at Gilgamesh's *ius primae noctis*? If so, hasn't he understood that this is a ritual act sanctioned by the gods? *Is* the act sanctioned by the gods, as the young man says, or is this statement propaganda issuing from a sexually predatory tyrant? (We know that the gods have sent Enkidu to balance Gilgamesh's oppression, but we don't know the precise nature of that oppression. It is entirely possible that Gilgamesh, as the embodiment of the divine male principle, does have the right to sleep with every bride on her wedding night, but that he is appropriating other young women as well. It is also possible, as some scholars think, that the oppression has nothing sexual about it, that Gilgamesh, as a gigantic superjock, has been exhausting the men in athletic contests, and the women are worn out from taking care of them.) Finally, if the young man's report is accurate and if Enkidu has understood it correctly, is he rebelling against the divine order? Or, alternatively, does he accept the divine order and simply want to replace Gilgamesh as the stud planting his seed in the virgins of Uruk? We simply don't know.

This not-knowing is an interesting position to be in as a reader. (It will become even more interesting in the monster-slaying episode of Books III–V.) One thing it means is that we don't take sides. Yes, Gilgamesh is a tyrant, but he is also magnificent. Yes, he mates with the lawful wife, but this apparent sexual predation may be in the divine order of things, and to oppose it is not necessarily virtuous. Every negative about him is balanced by a positive. Of course, from another perspective, it is clear that the whole world of Uruk is out of balance because of Gilgamesh's manic excesses and that Enkidu has been created to restore that balance. It is equally clear that the confrontation between the two heroes is not going to be a struggle between good and evil. There are too many ambiguities here for the mind to settle in a position of moral certainty. This leaves us with the raw emotion of Enkidu's anger, which, unexplained and uninterpretable, serves to move him from the shepherds' huts to the great city.

As Enkidu enters Uruk, he is mobbed like a celebrity. He may be gigantic, he may have a savage past, but he is fully human now, and, recognizing his innocence, people are not too frightened to approach him, as the trapper was. The crowds treat him with a mixture of awe and tenderness, marveling at his enormous body and kissing his enormous feet as if they were doting mothers kissing the most luscious morsels of infant flesh. Enkidu finds his way to the marriage house and plants himself in front of the door, immovable.

When Gilgamesh arrives, the two heroes seize each other, butting heads like wild bulls, careening through the streets, crashing into walls, and making the houses tremble. The confrontation could hardly be more primal, stripped down to the element of male pride. Enkidu's anger is beside the point. There are no principles to be upheld, no justifications and counterjustifications. The battle is as silly as a schoolyard fight, yet there is something beautiful about its energy. There is also a deeply erotic element in it. This is not a fight to the death, as in the *Iliad* or *Beowulf.* It is a fight at the end of which each man will be able to say to his opponent, "Now I know you," or even (as Jacob said to his angel), "I will not let thee go, except thou bless me." It is an entrance into intimacy, and as close to lovemaking as to violence.

The poem comes just short of stating that the relationship between Gilgamesh and Enkidu is homosexual (in Tablet XII, a separate poem appended to the epic, the genital sexuality is explicit). But it's clear that the homoerotic element in their bond is very strong. Even before he meets Enkidu in combat, Gilgamesh dreams of him in an image of great physical tenderness. A boulder representing Enkidu falls from the sky; at first it is too heavy to budge, then it becomes the beloved in his arms, stone turning to warm flesh through the power of the metaphor. Gilgamesh's mother, in interpreting the dream, says that that is indeed how it will be, that the boulder

"stands for a dear friend, a mighty hero.
You will take him in your arms, embrace and caress him
the way a man caresses his wife."

Both men come to feel their friendship as a kind of marriage, and each one could say, as David says of Jonathan, "Thy love to me [is] wonderful, passing the love of women."

After the fight, Enkidu doesn't slink off or proffer his neck like an animal defeated by the alpha male; in a speech of the loveliest, most dignified humility, he acknowledges Gilgamesh as the superior fighter, the superior human being. In fact, he sees him with the eyes of appreciation, gazing at him in wonder as Shamhat had advised him to.

"Gilgamesh, you are unique among humans.
Your mother, the goddess Ninsun, made you
stronger and braver than any mortal,
and rightly has Enlil* granted you the kingship,
since you are destined to rule over men."

Gilgamesh, as victor, doesn't feel the need to reciprocate with any appreciation of Enkidu. But he knows that what he dreamed at the end of Book I has come true. The dear friend and mighty hero has appeared, the longed-for companion of his heart, the man who

---

* Enlil, along with Anu and Ea, is one of the triumvirate of great gods who govern the universe.

will stand at his side through the greatest dangers. The fight is over without any residue of anger, resentment, or competitiveness. They know each other through and through. Like David and Jonathan, each loves the other as his own soul.

A MONSTER IN THE HOUSE

So Gilgamesh and Enkidu become true friends. Now, because the two heroes "balance each other perfectly," Uruk can have peace. Now the son can return to his father, the girl can return to her mother, and the life of the great city can continue in all its vibrancy, with no shadow of oppression to make the people cry out. The two realities can collapse into Shamhat's enamored vision of a truly civilized, festive society of bright colors and finery and music and laughing courtesan-priestesses and gratified desire. The gods are in their heaven and, for the time being, all's right with the world.

The transition to the next episode—the journey to the Cedar Forest and the killing of the monster Humbaba—is fragmentary and obscure. We aren't told how long Gilgamesh and Enkidu stayed in Uruk deepening their friendship; we don't know what they did during those weeks or months. How do vigorous young giants spend their free time? This is not one of the poem's interests, but it's easy to imagine an ongoing revel of feasting and beer drinking, wrestling matches, swimming, polo, bullfighting perhaps, Gilgamesh delightedly teaching his friend all the new dances and songs, daily visits to the Eanna temple to make love with the most beautiful of the young priestesses (Shamhat included), and—because ancient Babylonian kings prided themselves on being scholars as well as warriors and athletes—daily visits to the royal library, where Enkidu can take lessons in elementary cuneiform.

At a certain point, though, out of the blue, Gilgamesh announces that it is time to leave Uruk and begin the fatal adventure that provides the shape for the rest of the epic: an ascent to an ambiguous victory, followed by a plunge into death, unassuageable grief, and the futile search for immortality. "Now we must travel to the Cedar Forest," Gilgamesh says,

> "where the fierce monster Humbaba lives.
> We must kill him and drive out evil from the world."

Living in the year 2004, one can't help hearing this statement of an ancient Mesopotamian king in eerie counterpoint to the recent American invasion of Iraq. From this perspective, Gilgamesh's action is the original preemptive attack. Ancient readers, like many contemporary Americans, would have considered it to be unquestionably heroic. But the poem is wiser than the culture from which it arose. It wonderfully complicates the ostensible moral certainties, and once again, when we look closely, the mind finds no solid ground to stand on.

What impels Gilgamesh to go on this adventure? Why should he kill the monster? At first, all we hear is the sudden announcement itself. As listeners to a great adventure story, we don't need any more motivation than this. After all, that's what heroes do: they slay monsters. The motivation in this sense is literary rather than psychological. Story, not character, is fate.

But a bit further on, the poet does provide a motivation for the decision to leave for the Cedar Forest. What Gilgamesh wants is fame, as he explains in a passionate speech to Enkidu:

"We are not gods, we cannot ascend
to heaven. No, we are mortal men.
Only the gods live forever. *Our* days
are few in number, and whatever we achieve
is a puff of wind. Why be afraid then,
since sooner or later death must come? . . .
I will cut down the tree, I will kill Humbaba,
I will make a lasting name for myself,
I will stamp my fame on men's minds forever."

It is obvious that Gilgamesh considers himself fully human and that, for him, "two-thirds divine" is just a polite compliment or a rhetorical flourish. His mother may be a goddess, but he is as mortal as any other human. The only way for him to transcend death, he thinks, is to make an everlasting name for himself.

The desire for fame is at the heart of the ancient heroic traditions, Babylonian, Greek, and Germanic. It is one of the nobler delusions, and it can produce great art—in addition, as we know, to great havoc. There is something very human and even endearing about all this posturing; human nature hasn't changed much from Gilgamesh— or Enkidu, with his *"I am the mightiest!"*—to Cassius Clay. But heroic? It's hard to take the boasts and the derring-do seriously in comparison with the actions of what we would all consider true heroes: those who risk harm or death for the sake of others. The anonymous, everyday heroism of fire fighters and police officers makes the desire for "a lasting name" seem far less admirable to us than it has seemed to other cultures. In any event, the poet makes it clear from the outset that however morally Gilgamesh thinks he is acting, he wants to kill Humbaba "and drive out evil from the world," not for the sake of the people, or to alleviate suffering, or to help any-one but himself.

As the story proceeds, we hear another possible motivation: that Shamash, the sun god, god of justice and Gilgamesh's special protector, has put this decision into his head. At least, that is the the-ory of Gilgamesh's mother, the goddess Ninsun (neither Gilgamesh nor Shamash ever acknowledges it). According to her, the whole adventure is Shamash's idea, and Gilgamesh is only an instrument in his hand, a warrior in the battle of good against evil. "Lord of heaven," Ninsun says in her prayer to the sun god,

> "you have granted my son
> beauty and strength and courage—why
> have you burdened him with a restless heart?
> Now you have stirred him up to attack
> the monster Humbaba, to make a long
> journey from which he may not return.
> Since he has resolved to go, protect him
> until he arrives at the Cedar Forest,

until he kills the monster Humbaba
and drives from the world the evil that you hate."

Here Ninsun, "the wise, the all-knowing," is portrayed as a purely
human figure, neither more nor less wise than any worried mother
of flesh and blood. She knows her son well, and when she mentions
his "restless heart," she is pointing to what drives Gilgamesh
throughout the epic, both before and after Enkidu's death. What-
ever Shamash's part in the process may be, we can understand how
Gilgamesh's restless heart has stirred him up, as powerfully as his
desire for fame. Psychologically, this restlessness can't be inspired by
the god of justice; it is the opposite of inspiration; it is ultimately
desperation. One might even say that the attack on Humbaba stems
from what Pascal called the cause of all human misery: the inability
to sit contentedly alone in a room.

Is Ninsun correct in her theory that this is a battle of good
against evil? Everything in the poem argues against it. As a matter of
fact, the only evil we are informed of is the suffering Gilgamesh has
inflicted on his own people; the only monster is Gilgamesh himself.*
If he has a real enemy, it is the selfishness that arises from his own
restless heart. Uruk may be at peace now, but Gilgamesh isn't. The

---

* This is not counting the separable Bull of Heaven episode of Book VI,
which contains two monsters, Ishtar and the Bull, or the story-within-a-
story of Book XI, in which the great gods send the Flood in a fit of genoci-
dal monstrosity.

moral imbalance still exists; he is, as far as we are told, unable to acknowledge what he has done, unable to apologize or make amends to the young men and women he has been terrorizing.

Whatever Gilgamesh's mother may say, the poet makes it impossible to see Humbaba as a threat to the security of Uruk or as part of any "axis of evil." Unlike Grendel in *Beowulf,* he is not seen as the enemy of God; there is no devil or negative metaphysical force in the poet's cosmology for him to be an instrument of. He hasn't harmed a single living being, as far as we know. If anything, our sympathies are with him. He may be ugly and terrifying, with his fire-spewing breath, thunderous voice, and nightmare faces, but to be terrifying is his job. He just stays where he is, minding his business and doing his duty, which is to take care of the Cedar Forest and keep humans out. "If anyone knows the rules of my forest," he says later to Enkidu,

> "it is you. You know that this is my place
> and that I am the forest's guardian. Enlil
> put me here to terrify men,
> and I guard the forest as Enlil ordains."

Like the precivilized Enkidu, Humbaba is a figure of balance and a defender of the ecosystem. (Having a monster or two around to guard our national forests from corporate and other predators wouldn't be such a bad thing.)

I love how the poet has morally situated his poem so that as soon as we are tempted to take a position about good and evil, we realize

that there is an opposite and equally valid position. This world, like ours, is not black and white; there is ultimately nowhere to stand, no side we can ultimately take and not cut ourselves off from the truth. Yes, Humbaba is a monster; perhaps he is evil, as Ninsun says; conceivably he is even a threat to the city, though we are never told how. But it is at least as true that Humbaba has his appointed place in the divine order of things. He has specifically been commissioned to be monstrous by one of the great gods, because humans are not supposed to penetrate into the Cedar Forest and chop down its trees.

If there must be a monster in-the house (to paraphrase Wallace Stevens), let him be one who is just doing his job, without malice. The problem with believing in evil monsters and an evil-hating god (or God) is that it splits the universe down the middle, separates us from at least half of creation, and eventually leads to the claustrophobic and doom-haunted world of the Germanic hero sagas, however idealistic we may be. "The struggle between good and evil / is the primal disease of the mind," wrote the sixth-century Zen master Seng-ts'an, who knew what he was talking about. It is all too easy to see ourselves as fighting on God's side, to identify our ideology with what is best for the world and use it to justify crusades, pogroms, or preemptive attacks. Projecting evil onto the world makes me unassailably right—a position as dangerous in politics as in marriage.

Much of Book III is in debate form: between Gilgamesh and Enkidu, then between Gilgamesh and the elders of Uruk. It is a debate between bravery (or foolhardiness) and prudence. Gilgamesh's position is that he must go on this journey in order to win everlasting fame. Enkidu first points out that the Cedar Forest is forbidden to humans and that Humbaba has been put there by Enlil himself, to terrify men. Then, echoed by the elders, he says that in any case the journey is too dangerous and Humbaba too powerful. The arguments are not sophisticated and don't vary. Gilgamesh wins the debate by walking away. He is the king, after all, and can do whatever he wants; what he wants now is to order new weapons at the forge. By the end of the episode, Enkidu and the whole city support him. The elders offer their cautious, geriatric advice. The young men cheer. The heroes depart.

They walk east, in three-day marches, at the pace of more than three hundred miles a day (not a huge effort for someone like Gilgamesh, whose legs, according to one fragmentary passage, are nine feet long). Each march is described in exactly the same way; the repetition creates a sense of extended time, a shift from the ordinary time of the city into mythological time. Each culminates in the dream ritual, which is described in the same few crisply visualized lines. Gilgamesh's dreams vary in their details, but they are all essentially the same dream of disaster or near disaster. Enkidu, by the method known as "reversal of values," interprets them as omens that promise victory. And though his interpretation is correct for the actual battle with Humbaba, there is another sense in which the dreams are begging to be taken at their face value, unreversed, as the other dreams in the epic are. A disaster does indeed loom ahead, though with a time delay. Ironically, it involves the death of the dream interpreter, a death that is the direct, divinely ordained consequence of killing Humbaba. A more literal interpreter might advise Gilgamesh to turn back, however aggressively Shamash urges him to attack.

Inside the Cedar Forest, Gilgamesh and Enkidu are alternately seized by terror, and each in turn encourages the other. For a Babylonian hero, unlike the imperviously brave men of Germanic legends, like Beowulf and Siegfried, it was no disgrace to feel fear. Gilgamesh can not only be afraid at the sight of the monster, but can say he is. He does not run like the great Hector fleeing in terror from Achilles outside the wall of Troy, but he is frozen in his tracks. Enkidu, who previously was so reluctant to proceed, now urges Gilgamesh not to retreat, and they walk on to the monster's den.

The battle is over quickly. Humbaba is about to overwhelm the two heroes when Shamash sends mighty winds that pin him down and paralyze him. This divine intervention may strike us as rather unfair, but a world in which the gods take sides is not a meritocracy.

With Gilgamesh on top of him, holding a knife to his throat, Humbaba begs both heroes for mercy. These passages are at once comic and poignant: comic in the disproportion between the monster's previous threats and his present abasement, and poignant in the humility and reasonableness of his request. It is an extraordinary moment—think how impossible it would be in *Beowulf* for a monster to refer to the concept of mercy or for the hero even to consider it. One can't help feeling a surge of sympathy for the doomed Humbaba.

Gilgamesh hesitates. We are not told why, but it is probable that, like his predecessor in the Sumerian poem "Gilgamesh and Huwawa,"

"Gilgamesh's noble heart took pity on" the monster. Enkidu, though, has no doubts. Three separate times he urges his friend to kill the guardian of the Cedar Forest, even though he is aware that killing him will enrage not only Enlil but their own protector Shamash as well. (Thus, as it turns out, Ninsun, "the wise, the all-knowing," was mistaken in her opinion that Humbaba is an evil thing that Shamash wants to have destroyed. Defeated, yes; destroyed, no.)

> "Dear friend, quickly,
> before another moment goes by,
> kill Humbaba, don't listen to his words,
> don't hesitate, slaughter him, slit his throat,
> before the great god Enlil can stop us,
> before the great gods can get enraged,
> Enlil in Nippur, Shamash in Larsa.
> Establish your fame, so that forever
> men will speak of brave Gilgamesh,
> who killed Humbaba in the Cedar Forest."

Enkidu, it seems, has by now completely taken on Gilgamesh's warrior ethos, the desire for fame superseding every other consideration. True, it is his friend's fame, not his own, that he wants to establish. But generous as it may be, this love is still an *égoïsme à deux*; it has simply replaced *I am the mightiest!* with *You are the mightiest!* And in its disregard for mercy, prudence, and cosmic hierarchy, it creates disaster.

The principle that every action has an effect is not something

that Gilgamesh or Enkidu can be expected to know (as heroes, they need to be strong and brave, not insightful). But the poet, as we will see, is aware of it; he is too intelligent not to know that monster-slaying expeditions, even the most well-intentioned ones, have unforeseen and potentially disastrous consequences. Enkidu is morally responsible for persuading his friend not to spare the monster's life; therefore his own life becomes forfeit. When Gilgamesh kills Humbaba, the poet says, a gentle rain falls onto the mountains, as if the heavens themselves are weeping for the consequences of that act.

HUMILIATING
THE GODDESS

Almost all the female characters in *Gilgamesh*—Shamhat, Ninsun, Shiduri, and Utnapishtim's wife—are portrayed as admirable: intelligent, generous, compassionate. The one exception is Ishtar, goddess of love and patron deity of Uruk. In the very peculiar and invigorating Book VI, she is rejected, insulted, threatened, and humiliated by both Gilgamesh and Enkidu. This is surprising in a poem that mentions her temple with reverence and makes one of her priestesses a central character in the initial drama. It is even more surprising in light of the goddess's millennia-old position in Mesopotamian culture: she was known to the Sumerians as Inanna, the Queen of Heaven, and "played a greater role in myth, epic, and hymn than any other deity, male or female." Anyone who has first read the beautiful, tender, marvelously erotic song cycle called "The Courtship of Inanna and Dumuzi" is likely to feel flabbergasted at the shabby treatment Ishtar receives at the hand of the *Gilgamesh* poet.

But there is another side to the beloved goddess who brought culture and fertility to her people in Sumer. She is also the goddess of war, and she can be selfish, arbitrary, and brutal. In the Sumerian poem "The Descent of Inanna," she "fastens the eye of death" on her husband, Dumuzi (Tammuz), and orders him to be dragged down to hell by two persistent demons. In a lesser-known poem called "Inanna and Ebih," which begins with an invocation to the "goddess of the dreadful powers, clad in terror, drenched in blood," she destroys an entire mountain range because it doesn't show her enough respect. Sumerian literature furnishes other examples of her ruthlessness.

Why the *Gilgamesh* poet chose to focus so exclusively on Ishtar's dark side in Book VI and to portray his heroes as so vituperative is a mystery. No scholar has provided an adequate explanation of whatever cultural forces were at work behind the episode. Is it symptomatic of a religious movement among first the Sumerians and later the Babylonians to displace her with a male deity? Then why are her priestesses treated with such respect? And how can we explain the poet's irreverence to the gods in general, who are later compared to dogs and flies? We just don't know. All we can do is enjoy the episode and see how it fits into the poem as a whole.

Things begin calmly enough. Gilgamesh, having returned from the Cedar Forest, washes himself and gets dressed in his magnificent royal robes. He is looking mighty fine. Ishtar sees him and falls in love,

or lust. In a speech that seems forward or straightforward, depending on one's cultural bias, she propositions him, offering him an array of fabulous gifts if only he will be her lover.

Gilgamesh's rejection is at first polite, even tactful. But it soon changes into a series of metaphorical insults, all of which accuse Ishtar of damaging the very person whom she should have been caring for. Next, he cites six famous love affairs of Ishtar's—with Tammuz, then with the roller bird, the lion, the stallion, the shepherd, and the gardener Ishullanu (her taste in lovers is species-transcendent, omnisexual)—all of them black-widow affairs in which she turned against her lover and harmed him. Gilgamesh concludes by saying that if he were to accept her offer, she would treat him as cruelly as she treated them.

It is a remarkably vivid speech, the longest in the poem except for Utnapishtim's account of the Flood. Reading it, we are caught up in the pure energy of the insults. It is like a tribal dance in which lines of young men and young women advance in turn and fling ritual taunts at each other. The speech's climax, the catalogue of lovers, is a miniature *Metamorphoses* that casts Ishtar as Circe and moves from disaster to disaster, not only with the satisfaction of a lawyer proving his case, but also with the delight of a storyteller. Aside from the affair with Tammuz, we are ignorant of the myths the poet is referring to (they haven't survived in Sumerian or Akkadian literature); for modern readers this gives the passage a certain piquancy, as if we were overhearing intimate stories about people we don't know.

Is Gilgamesh's response inappropriate? Is it a frightened male reaction to a woman who takes the sexual initiative? Perhaps, though

that would be odd in a poem that celebrates a character like Shamhat. But from the above-mentioned "Descent of Inanna," we can be sure that in at least one of his six examples, Gilgamesh is giving us accurate information. Sleeping with Ishtar can be dangerous to your health. And when we witness her violent response to his rejection, we tend to think that he has been entirely reasonable in just saying no.

The next scene is a portrait of Ishtar as a murderous spoiled brat. She explodes with tears of rage and frustration, goes to Anu, father of the gods, and throws a tantrum until he lends her the Bull of Heaven to kill Gilgamesh and destroy his palace. As a woman scorned, Ishtar is not only petulant and vengeful; she is a real monster, willing to sacrifice hundreds of people for the sake of her revenge.

But Enkidu and Gilgamesh make short work of the gigantic Bull. They are fearless; there is none of the hauntedness and wavering of the Humbaba episode. There isn't even a feeling of danger, in spite of the Bull's first two warrior-demolishing snorts. The action is swift, the humor coarse, and the killing of the Bull seems less a battle than a sport. In its grace of movement, it is like the roughly contemporaneous bull-leaping fresco in the palace of Knossos on Crete, in which an athlete has leaped over the bull's horns and, arms gripping its sides, legs dangling above his head, is about to flip over its haunch onto the ground.

Ishtar is brought to helpless tears by her failure. Standing on top of the city wall, she cries out,

> "Not only did Gilgamesh
> slander me—now the brute has killed
> his own punishment, the Bull of Heaven."

This is funny, but with an uncomfortable kind of humor that depends on the humiliation of the villain. (How many of us nowadays can enjoy Shylock's anguished, ridiculous cry "My daughter! O my ducats! O my daughter!"?) Even when the villainess has just murdered three hundred people, one doesn't like to take pleasure in her pain.

Enkidu, however, is not so delicate:

> When Enkidu heard these words, he laughed,
> he reached down, ripped off one of the Bull's
> thighs, and flung it in Ishtar's face.
> "If only I could catch you, this is what
> I would do to you, I would rip *you* apart
> and drape the Bull's guts over your arms!"

Here again, as in the killing of Humbaba, Enkidu is the more extreme of the two friends. As with the hero's ethic, he has gotten on Gilgamesh's high horse and ridden it so far that Gilgamesh seems almost temperate in comparison. This final heaping of insult upon insult, as energizing as it is shocking in its hubris and sheer outrageousness, is clearly dangerous, especially when your opponent is a goddess. What makes it so grotesquely funny is the combination of innocence and cruelty, in which there is more than a passing resemblance between Ishtar and the two heroes.

Later that day, after the victory parade, when Gilgamesh boasts and does his victory strut, he reminds us of a champion athlete who not only crushes his opponent but flips him the bird:

> "Tell me: Who is the handsomest of men?
> Tell me: Who is the bravest of heroes?
> Gilgamesh—he is the handsomest of men,
> Enkidu—he is the bravest of heroes.
> We are the victors who in our fury
> flung the Bull's thigh in Ishtar's face,
> and now, in the streets, she has no one to avenge her."

There are more intelligent ways to return home after a death that you know has enraged the great gods.

If the psychological task of the hero is to gain mastery over the internal monsters by killing the external ones, Gilgamesh has been radically unsuccessful. Killing Humbaba and the Bull has given him no greater control over himself and his own arrogance. Enkidu's arrival may have provided some balance for him; at least he has stopped oppressing the citizens of Uruk. But if the gods expected that Enkidu would provide peace for the king as well as for the city, they are sadly mistaken. Gilgamesh will have to learn limits another way.

It is obvious that Book VI is a separable episode that could be omitted without any loss of continuity. The heroes kill Humbaba in Book V, and in the death of Enkidu at the end of Book VII they suffer the results of their act. But the progression to tragedy would seem abrupt without the Ishtar episode. Book VI is a comic interlude, like the satyr play that was performed after Greek tragedies: obscene, vulgar, high-spirited, irreverent, and rambunctious, letting loose all the energies that will soon enough become contained and very somber.

DEATH AND DEPARTURE

Suddenly Enkidu has two dreams about dying. The second of them gives us a wonderfully graphic picture of how the ancient Mesopotamians imagined the dead, who sit miserably in pitch darkness, "dressed in feathered garments like birds." The great gods are not mocked, and the killing of Humbaba will have fatal consequences. Gilgamesh, through his tears, calls the first dream nonsense and makes a weak attempt to interpret the second one as a good omen. But both friends know that Enkidu is doomed. And indeed, as his dreams warned, he falls mortally ill.

The next morning, Enkidu curses the trapper, and then Shamhat, for taking him out of the wilderness. (It never occurs to him to curse his beloved Gilgamesh as well, though this was Gilgamesh's idea.) The speech expresses Enkidu's impotence at the thought of dying, and part of its power is in letting out all the stops on the vindictive, outward-blaming ego. "May wild dogs camp in your bedroom," Enkidu says,

> "may owls
> nest in your attic, may drunkards vomit
> all over you, may a tavern wall
> be your place of business, may you be dressed
> in torn robes and filthy underwear,
> may angry wives sue you, may thorns and briars
> make your feet bloody, may young men jeer
> and the rabble mock you as you walk the streets."

The speech is not just a rant; it is also powerful reporting, once we transpose the optative to the indicative: a portrait of the life of an aging prostitute, with its poverty, abuse, and humiliation.

Shamash provides Enkidu with a more balanced view that calms his "raging heart." Civilization, the god points out, has been just as much a paradise for Enkidu as the wilderness was. And wasn't it Shamhat who brought Enkidu the greatest joy of all, his friendship with Gilgamesh? Enkidu acknowledges this and turns his curse of Shamhat into a blessing. "May you be adored by nobles and princes," he says; "may Ishtar give you generous lovers / whose treasure chests brim with jewels and gold." In the interval between the curse and the blessing, Shamhat has ascended from the cheapest of whores to the most expensive and esteemed of courtesans, a kind of Babylonian Ninon de Lenclos. Oddly, both curse and blessing imagine Shamhat as a prostitute (poor or rich) rather than a priestess; Enkidu doesn't seem to know the difference. Of course, it is possible that many priestesses of Ishtar would have been delighted to be wealthy courtesans instead. But for the true devotee, the change would hardly have been a blessing. Devotion to the goddess was at the core of her life, and in comparison, even the kind of wealth and adulation given to a Hollywood star would have been meaningless.

After twelve days of agony, Enkidu dies and leaves Gilgamesh alone with his grief. It is a tragic moment in the epic, though epics are not necessarily tragic; the Homeric poems contain both the tragedy of Achilles and the romance of Odysseus, with its happy ending (for him, if not for the suitors and the little dangling maids). Enkidu could easily be seen as a tragic hero, pulled out of his Eden into the corrupt world of humans to suffer an arbitrary death sentence from the gods. And, as reconciled as he seems, there is a certain lingering bitterness about his death. One might say that his death was caused by Gilgamesh's monster-hunting, just as his birth was caused by Gilgamesh's tyranny. But more accurately, Enkidu caused his own death by insisting that Gilgamesh kill Humbaba; if they had let the monster live, all would have been well. The fact that neither Enkidu nor Gilgamesh ever realizes this is part of the pathos of the situation.

Gilgamesh's lament at the beginning of Book VIII is one of the most beautiful elegies in literature. In it he asks both the natural world and the world of the city to join him as he mourns his friend. The simple, repeated phrases of his lament are exquisitely sorrowful.

"My beloved friend is dead, he is dead,
my beloved brother is dead, I will mourn

as long as I breathe, I will sob for him
like a woman who has lost her only child."

Gilgamesh's grief is too intense for any understanding to pene-
trate. There is no way, in spite of Enkidu's first dream, that he can
make a causal connection between the killing of Humbaba and
Enkidu's death. For him, the events just occurred, one after the other,
and he can still boast of the killings, unconscious that they have cost
him his beloved friend. Indeed, the music of his grief is so enchanting
that, for the time being, we don't even want him to understand.

"Beloved friend, swift stallion, wild deer,
leopard ranging in the wilderness—
Enkidu, my friend, swift stallion, wild deer,
leopard ranging in the wilderness—
together we crossed the mountains, together
we slaughtered the Bull of Heaven, we killed
Humbaba, who guarded the Cedar Forest."

Actually, he is in a trance of pain: even if he could understand
why Enkidu died, it wouldn't matter; the brute fact of the event would
blot out any other consideration. He is so overwhelmed by the sight
of Enkidu's lifeless body that, a dozen lines after lamenting that his
friend is dead, he can no longer even find a name for death. As a great
warrior, he has seen and caused many deaths. But now, for the first
time, death is an intimate reality, and he can barely recognize it.

"O Enkidu, what is this sleep that has seized you,
that has darkened your face and stopped your breath?"

Even though he has been up all night, sobbing for Enkidu, he can't let himself know what has happened. It's as if he has never seen a corpse before. He reacts like a young child, or like an animal sniffing at the dead body of its mate, bewildered. He half-expects Enkidu to answer. When he touches Enkidu's heart, he seems surprised that it isn't beating.

It takes a while longer for Gilgamesh to finally acknowledge that his friend is dead. But even then, his first gesture is to make death into a kind of marriage. He can't help treating Enkidu as if he were still alive and in mortal danger; after being the desolate bridegroom, he becomes the anxious mother.

Then he veiled Enkidu's face like a bride's.
Like an eagle Gilgamesh circled around him,
he paced in front of him, back and forth,
like a lioness whose cubs are trapped in a pit,
he tore out clumps of his hair, tore off
his magnificent robes as though they were cursed.

Finally, it's over. Gilgamesh orders a magnificent votive statue of Enkidu; he goes through all the necessary rituals to ensure that the gods of the underworld will welcome him and help him to "be peaceful and not sick at heart." But the ritual gestures, though meticulous, seem desperate. At best, Enkidu will be one of those miserable dirt-eating human birds who squat or shuffle in utter darkness, forever. This is poor comfort. So, abandoning all his privileges and responsibilities, giving up his roles as warrior and king, reversing Enkidu's journey from wilderness to civilization, Gilgamesh puts on an animal skin and leaves Uruk.

His departure is reminiscent of another royal departure a thousand years later, in the legend of the Buddha. Like Gilgamesh, Gotama, the future Awakened One, is transfixed by a vision of human vulnerability and feels compelled to leave his palace and all his possessions behind, so that he can search for the secret of life and death. Gotama's grief is not personal, though; he hasn't lost a beloved friend; he hasn't lost anyone except himself, his own identity. When, for the first time in his sheltered life, he sees sickness, old age, and death, his whole idea of what it is to be human, what it is that someday awaits him, collapses, and he is plunged into a desperate questioning. His story has a happier ending than Gilgamesh's: after six years of futile austerities, he sits down under the Bodhi tree, determined not to move until either death or understanding comes, and at dawn, when the morning star appears, suddenly he wakes up from the dream of suffering. "When you see the unborn, uncreated, unconditioned," he later said, "you are liberated from everything born, created, and conditioned."

Gilgamesh too asks an all-consuming question about life and death. But his question is not driven by a deep need for understanding; it is driven by fear. (Rilke called *Gilgamesh* "the epic of the fear of death.") Fear is the reverse side of the cool warrior ethos, in which the consciousness of mortality motivates the hero to establish his fame. *"Our* days are few in number," Gilgamesh had said, imperturbably. "Why be afraid then, / since sooner or later death must come?" Why indeed? Except that terror comes unbidden, on the way to monsters or in the presence of overwhelming loss. Love has changed everything; it has made Gilgamesh absolutely vulnerable. His earlier consciousness of mortality turns out to be a pale, abstract thing in comparison with the anguish he feels as he roams though the wilderness.

> "Must I die too? Must I be as lifeless
> as Enkidu? How can I bear this sorrow
> that gnaws at my belly, this fear of death
> that restlessly drives me onward? If only
> I could find the one man whom the gods made immortal,
> I would ask him how to overcome death."

In his previous, heroic mode, Gilgamesh thought he knew that only the gods live forever. Now, terrified, he is no longer certain. His first question—"Must I die too?"—is not rhetorical; he really doesn't know the answer anymore. It is the question of a child at the threshold of adult awareness, who for the first time is faced with the concept of dying. Every child, to *become* an adult, must realize that the answer to that question is yes. (Once he has passed through the gate of "I will die," he can later, if his questioning goes deep enough, pass through the gate of "I was never born.")

Gilgamesh wants to find the one exception to the rule of mortality, his ancestor Utnapishtim, who was granted eternal life and dwells somewhere at the eastern edge of the world. The fact that there has been one exception to the rule of mortality means that there may be a second exception. This hope postpones Gilgamesh's necessary acceptance until a time when he is more ready for it, less raw with grief. Like a thousand later heroes in folktales and Zen stories, he sets out in search of a teacher who can give him wisdom. In this he is bound to be disappointed. Wisdom isn't an object; it can't be grasped by words, nor can it be passed on. But until Gilgamesh completes his quest, he won't be able to realize the futility of it. "This thing we tell of can never be found by seeking," said the Sufi master Abu Yazid al-Bistami, "yet only seekers find it."

The first arrival we hear about is at the Twin Peaks, two high mountains overlooking the tunnel into which the sun sets for its nightly underground journey and out of which it rises in the morning. Two terrifying monsters called "scorpion people" guard the eastern end of this tunnel, just as Humbaba guarded the Cedar Forest. After Gilgamesh recovers from his dread and approaches them (he is no longer in a monster-slaying frame of mind), the creatures turn out to be quite courteous and tell him that the road to Utnapishtim lies through the tunnel. The scorpion man, at his wife's compassionate urging, allows Gilgamesh to enter the tunnel, warning him that if he fails to get to the western end before the sun enters, he will be burned to a crisp. For twelve hours, nonstop, Gilgamesh runs through the pitch blackness, and he exits just as the sun is setting.

This is a symbolic death and rebirth, in which he passes through the darkness of an underworld and emerges into the dazzling, *Arabian Nights*—like garden of the gods.

But in its effects, it is not much of a rebirth. Gilgamesh is the same anguished, violent man he was before. Indeed, when he meets Shiduri the tavern keeper, he looks so murderous that she runs into her tavern and locks herself in. Gilgamesh deals with this by threatening to smash down the door. Force is still his automatic reaction—the way he responds to the world.

Shiduri is a strange character: a matron, possibly a goddess, who brews beer in a tavern at the edge of the ocean, apparently for those rare customers who can outrace the sun. She is frightened but curious, and from the roof asks Gilgamesh questions about his appearance and his destination that are repeated later in the poem. Gilgamesh once again gives eloquent voice to his grief. "Shouldn't my heart be filled with anguish?" he cries out.

> "My friend, my brother, whom I loved so dearly,
> who accompanied me through every danger—
> Enkidu, my brother, whom I loved so dearly,
> who accompanied me through every danger—
> the fate of mankind has overwhelmed him.
> For six days I would not let him be buried,
> thinking, 'If my grief is violent enough,
> perhaps he will come back to life again.'
> For six days and seven nights I mourned him,

until a maggot fell out of his nose.
Then I was afraid, I was frightened by death,
and I set out to roam the wilderness.
I cannot bear what happened to my friend—
I cannot bear what happened to Enkidu—
so I roam the wilderness in my grief.
How can my mind have any rest?
My beloved friend has turned into clay—
my beloved Enkidu has turned into clay.
And won't I too lie down in the dirt
like him, and never arise again?"

This speech is as palpable and moving as his lament in Book VIII.

Shiduri sends him on to the next stage of his journey, but not before giving him a charming piece of conventional wisdom that can do him no earthly good. (No advice can. He needs to come to wisdom by himself.)

"Savor your food, make each of your days
a delight, bathe and anoint yourself,
wear bright clothes that are sparkling clean,
let music and dancing fill your house,
love the child who holds you by the hand,
and give your wife pleasure in your embrace.
That is the best way for a man to live."

But Gilgamesh is incapable of enjoyment; he must persevere until he finds Utnapishtim. Shiduri tells him that the only man who can help is Urshanabi, Utnapishtim's boatman. If Gilgamesh asks, perhaps Urshanabi will sail him across the vast ocean in his boat, crewed by the Stone Men, who are invulnerable to the Waters of Death.

Instead of being civil to the man on whom everything now depends, Gilgamesh proceeds with the senseless, self-defeating violence he is used to: he attacks Urshanabi and smashes the Stone Men to pieces. Fortunately for him, however, Urshanabi is a genial, forgiving fellow, who proposes an alternative method of crossing the Waters of Death, using punting poles instead of the demolished Stone Men. They sail "without stopping, for three days and nights, / a six weeks' journey for ordinary men," cross the Waters of Death, and finally land on the shore where Utnapishtim is waiting. Gilgamesh doesn't realize it yet, but he is standing face to face with the man who is his last hope.

WHEN THERE'S NO WAY OUT, YOU JUST FOLLOW THE WAY IN FRONT OF YOU

The archetypal hero's journey proceeds in stages: being called to action, meeting a wise man or guide, crossing the threshold into the numinous world of the adventure, passing various tests, attaining the goal, defeating the forces of evil, and going back home. It leads to a spiritual transformation at the end, a sense of gratitude, humility, and deepened trust in the intelligence of the universe. After he finds the treasure or slays the dragon or wins the princess or joins with the mind of the sage, the hero can return to ordinary life in a state of grace, as a blessing to himself and to his whole community. He has suffered, he has triumphed, he is at peace.

The more we try to fit *Gilgamesh* into the pattern of this archetypal journey, the more bizarre, quirky, and postmodern it seems. It is the original quest story. But it is also an anti-quest, since it undermines the quest myth from the beginning. Gilgamesh does slay the monster, but that, it turns out, is a violation of the divine order of things and causes the death of his beloved friend. He does journey to the edge of the world, he meets the wise man, but still there is no transformation. Utnapishtim asks him the same questions Shiduri asked, and Gilgamesh answers with the same anguished cries, whereupon Utnapishtim offers him yet another piece of conventional wisdom—beautiful words, but as useless to him as Shiduri's were. What's the good of saying, like everybody's obtuse uncle, that Gilgamesh should realize how fortunate he is, that life is short and death is final? It is like all well-meaning advice that tells us to accept things as they are. We *can't* accept things as they are, so long as we think that things should be different. Tell us how not to believe what we think, and then maybe we'll be able to hear.

In any case, for Utnapishtim to say that life is short is a bit disingenuous. Life *isn't* short—for him. That's the point! Why else has

Gilgamesh traveled to the edge of the world to see him? The desperate, grief-stricken man standing before Utnapishtim feels less fortunate than the very fool he is purportedly so superior to. He wants to transcend death, not accept it—right now, not in some happy future. There is no consolation in platitudes, and for Utnapishtim to tell him that he is going to die seems as tactless as it was for St. Paul to tell the Thessalonians that they were *not* going to die.

The only effect the speech seems to have is that Gilgamesh finally recognizes the old man as Utnapishtim. He also acts with a restraint that we haven't seen before. "I intended to fight you," he says,

> "yet now that I stand
> before you, now that I see who you are,
> I can't fight, something is holding me back."

Finally, Gilgamesh gets to ask his burning question: How did Utnapishtim overcome death and become immortal? Utnapishtim, who is not a believer in making a long story short, tells him about the Great Flood. His speech is a very strong piece of writing, as beautiful as its descendent, the Noah story, but far more detailed and dramatic, and filled with the most vivid images: the unsuspecting workmen drinking barrels of beer and wine to celebrate the completion of the ship; the terrified gods fleeing to the highest heaven and cowering there like dogs; Utnapishtim falling to his knees and weeping at the first touch of the blessed sunlight; the gods, starved because all their human food-providers have drowned, smelling the sweet fragrance of Utnapishtim's sacrifice and clustering around it like flies.

The Flood story explains Utnapishtim's exemption from mortality by narrating the circumstances that prompted the gods' decision. It also explains the Prologue's statement that Gilgamesh "had been granted a vision / into the great mystery, the secret places, / the primeval days before the Flood." The vision into the great mystery does not, however, seem to do Gilgamesh a bit of good, at least now. It certainly doesn't tell him how to overcome death. Immortality, it turns out, was a one-time offer, and that bleak fact is Utnapishtim's main revelation.

Why, then, did the poet include the Flood story at such length? Is it merely an interesting digression? Any reader who wants to understand its dramatic function in the poem should read Book XI again, this time skipping from Gilgamesh's first question ("Tell me, how is it that you, a mortal . . .") to the end of Utnapishtim's speech ("Now then, Gilgamesh, who will assemble . . . ?"). If you delete or drastically abridge the Flood story, the interval between the question and the dashing of Gilgamesh's hopes seems far too short. But with the story continuing for as long as it does, the suspense keeps growing. We are aware that Gilgamesh is listening with absolute attention, because at any moment the way to overcome death may be revealed. We can feel his attention even the second or tenth time we read this speech, when we know that Gilgamesh won't find his answer. And when the speech comes to its disappointing climax, we are carried on to the next incident with at least the satisfaction of knowing the whole story. We have heard everything there is to hear about how Utnapishtim became a god. Obviously, this is not the way out.

The story has another dramatic effect as well. It gives us a harrowing picture of the cost of Utnapishtim's immortality; the immortality itself seems like a pallid afterthought. Hovering in the background of this narrative is an unspoken question: If you had to experience all that terror, and the death of almost every living thing, in order to be granted immortality, would it seem worth it?

Far from being sympathetic to Gilgamesh's anguish, Utnapishtim is gruff, almost taunting, in the conclusion to his speech:

> "Now then, Gilgamesh, who will assemble
> the gods for *your* sake? Who will convince them
> to grant you the eternal life that you seek?"

(The more Utnapishtim reveals of his crankiness and cynicism, the less attractive immortality becomes.) He proposes a test: If Gilgamesh can overcome sleep for seven days—sleep being the likeness of death—perhaps he will be able to overcome death too. But Utnapishtim knows from the start that Gilgamesh, "worn out and ready to collapse," will fail the test. And indeed, he falls asleep immediately. Utnapishtim says with contempt:

> "Look at this fellow! He wanted to live
> forever, but the very moment he sat down,
> sleep swirled over him, like a fog."

There is a poignant irony about this test. In the bad old days, when Gilgamesh was terrorizing the citizens of Uruk, it was a well-known fact, as Shamhat told Enkidu, that the king was "so full of life-force that he need[ed] no sleep." Sometime after Enkidu's arrival he lost that vitality, in the same way that Enkidu, after he made love with Shamhat, lost his life-force and could no longer run like an animal. In this too Gilgamesh and Enkidu are twins. The poem doesn't tell us exactly when Gilgamesh began to need sleep. The first we hear of it is on the journey to the Cedar Forest, when it is a recurring element in the ritual for dreams.

> Gilgamesh sat there, with his chin on his knees,
> and sleep overcame him, as it does all men.

Experiencing intimacy seems to be for Gilgamesh what experiencing sex is for Enkidu: an initiation into human vulnerability. Once he found the companion of his heart, Gilgamesh became, in effect, three-thirds human. He left behind his kinship with the "unsleeping, undying" gods, just as Enkidu left behind the two-thirds of him that was animal. Unwittingly, each gave up part of his physical strength in order to know the kind of love that "an animal [or a god] can't know."

After Gilgamesh fails the test, Utnapishtim's wife, sweet where her husband is sour, suggests that they wake him up and gently send him back home. But according to Utnapishtim, Gilgamesh is a deceiver like all humans and must be shown proof that he slept, and this the seven hardening loaves provide. Gilgamesh, acknowledging his failure, cries out in a very moving and beautiful passage:

> "What shall I do,
> where shall I go now? Death has caught me,
> it lurks in my bedroom, and everywhere I look,
> everywhere I turn, there is only death."

After first making sure that Gilgamesh is washed and anointed, in a kind of ritual renewal, and is given royal robes that will stay clean until he returns to Uruk, Utnapishtim sends him on his way. And that seems to be the end of the story.

But Utnapishtim's compassionate wife intervenes once again. So, as a parting gift, Utnapishtim reveals a second secret of the gods. He tells Gilgamesh where, in the waters of the Great Deep (the freshwater sea under the earth), he can find a magical plant that will restore him to youth. However young his name implies he is, Gilgamesh feels old and weary now, and in desperate need of renewal. He plunges into the Great Deep, finds the plant, and brings it to the surface. Finally, it seems, he has found something that will put his heart at ease. But in this poem there is always a "but."

Gilgamesh's speech to Urshanabi the boatman on the shore of the Great Deep is a wonderfully complex little passage. First, he calls the marvelous plant "the antidote to the fear of death," and our questions begin. If eating the plant is not equivalent to passing the sleep test, but is a consolation prize instead—if it doesn't make you immortal like the fruit of the Tree of Life in the Garden of Eden— does it at least restore you to a protected youth in which you can't get fatally sick or injured, after which you again age and then die? Or is your youth just as vulnerable as an ordinary young person's? And when you grow old, can you take another bite and grow young a second time, a hundredth time, until the supply gives out? None of this is made clear; none of it has to be; any of it is possible. What *is* clear is that for someone who eats the plant, death has been temporarily avoided and the fear of death has been postponed. The plant is a medicine that addresses the symptoms of the fear of death, not its cause; it is a palliative, not a cure.

Still, Gilgamesh is elated. He tells Urshanabi that rather than eating the plant immediately, he first wants to test its effects:

> "I will take it to Uruk, I will test its power
> by seeing what happens when an old man eats it.
> If that succeeds, I will eat some myself
> and become a carefree young man again."

This statement too is complex and fascinating. Like the killing of Humbaba, it is first of all story-driven rather than character-driven. Gilgamesh must kill the monster because that's what heroes do; he must not eat the plant because, as we all know, he returns home aged and exhausted. But there are several possibilities implicit in his desire to take the plant home. Perhaps he is just being prudent (for the first time in his life). Perhaps he is afraid of the plant's effects, or at least cautious about them, and needs to use an old man in Uruk as a human guinea pig. On the other hand, it may not be prudence that motivates him to bring the plant home before eating it. Perhaps some transformation in his character has already begun, which makes him want to postpone the magical return to youth until he can do it in his own city, before the eyes of his own people. Perhaps there is also a desire to use the plant for the benefit of the whole community. He will go home, choose a particularly deserving old man who has nothing to lose by having the experiment fail, and if it succeeds, he will portion out tiny samples of the plant to a thousand old men, and give a sprig to the royal gardener to see if it can be cultivated in lush-gardened Uruk, so that it will be available for future generations as well. It is possible that something like these thoughts are taking shape in the shadowy recesses of Gilgamesh's mind.

So, without tasting the plant, he and Urshanabi head back to Uruk. The poet describes the trip in the same words that he used for the journey to the Cedar Forest: "At four hundred miles they stopped to eat, / at a thousand miles they pitched their camp." This is a reverse journey through the landscape of dreams; it is, in its formulaic language, the way back from the monster. But this time, it is not a return to hubris, violence, and death. It is a return to wholeness.

Still, there is one last failure to endure and overcome. On the way back, Gilgamesh bathes in a pond and, rather than handing the precious plant to Urshanabi, he leaves it on the ground. This act of stunning carelessness is like other famous last-minute mistakes in myths and folktales throughout the world (Orpheus' over-the-shoulder glance at Eurydice, for example, or the youngest son's choice to sit on the edge of a well in the Grimms' "The Golden Bird"). There is always something fated about these mistakes; they don't seem like accidents, because they are willed by the shape of the story; we feel that they had to happen. In light of Gilgamesh's history of violence and self-destruction, it seems that some inner dynamic won't allow him to eat the plant—that would be too simple, too good to be true. The spoiler is a snake, as in the Eden story, though here the snake is not cunning, it is entirely innocent and simply takes advantage of a good opportunity. The poet needs only three lines to shatter Gilgamesh's hopes:

> A snake smelled its fragrance, stealthily
> it crawled up and carried the plant away.
> As it disappeared, it cast off its skin.

Thus, in the words of Psalm 103, the snake's mouth is "satisfied with good things," and its "youth is renewed like the eagle's." O felix serpens!

When Gilgamesh realizes that the snake has slithered off with his antidote, he cries out yet again:

> "What shall I do now? All my hardships
> have been for nothing. O Urshanabi,

was it for this that my hands have labored,
was it for this that I gave my heart's blood?"

It is the last gasp of tragedy. One is touched by his anguish, but only so far. One also wants to say, Well, what do you expect, you silly goose?—that's what happens when you leave magic plants lying on the ground!

This is not the point, of course. The episode is not meant to be a lesson in prudence. It is the end of the line for Gilgamesh's quest. He is face to face with the realization that there is no immortality and no return to youth: a realization that can result (depending on your readiness) in either despair or freedom. When there's no way out, you just follow the way in front of you.

That way, for Gilgamesh, leads back home. And on the way home, in the course of the hundreds of miles he and Urshanabi travel every day, in the dream time that is left in total silence, an astonishing thing happens: Gilgamesh becomes one with the poet's voice. In spite of the Prologue's statement, we have never believed that Gilgamesh wrote the poem; he has always been a character in the story, not the narrator of it: a part of it, not the whole. Only now, for the first time, as Gilgamesh addresses Urshanabi with the same words that Sîn-lēqi-unninni addressed us with at the beginning of the poem, can we hear this authorial voice for ourselves.

When at last they arrived, Gilgamesh
said to Urshanabi, "This is
the wall of Uruk, which no city on earth can equal.

See how its ramparts gleam like copper in the sun.
Climb the stone staircase, more ancient than the mind
    can imagine,
approach the Eanna Temple, sacred to Ishtar,
a temple that no king has equaled in size or beauty,
walk on the wall of Uruk, follow its course
around the city, inspect its mighty foundations,
examine its brickwork, how masterfully it is built,
observe the land it encloses: the palm trees, the gardens,
the orchards, the glorious palaces and temples, the shops
and marketplaces, the houses, the public squares."

And that is how the poem ends: where it began. Its form is not circular, like *Finnegans Wake,* but spiral, since it begins again at another level, with Gilgamesh narrating. His transformation has taken place offstage, outside the frame of the poem, at the last possible moment. When we return to the beginning, where Gilgamesh's echoing lines point us, it is clear that he has completed the final stage of the archetypal hero's journey, in which the hero gives new life to his community, returning to them with the gifts he has discovered on his adventure.

He brought back the ancient, forgotten rites,
restoring the temples that the Flood had destroyed,
renewing the statutes and sacraments
for the welfare of the people and the sacred land.

We are not told how he learned "the ancient, forgotten rites" from Utnapishtim. But we know that for the first time he is acting as a responsible, compassionate king, a benefactor to his people and their descendents. Out of the depths, somehow, Gilgamesh has managed to "close the gate of sorrow"; he has learned how to rule himself and his city without violence, selfishness, or the compulsions of a restless heart.

Gilgamesh's quest is not an allegory. It is too subtle and rich in minute particulars to fit any abstract scheme. But issuing as it does from a deep level of human experience, it has a certain allegorical resonance. We don't need to be aware of this resonance in order to enjoy the story. Yet it is there.

When Gilgamesh leaves his city and goes into uncharted territory in search of a way beyond death, he is looking for something that is impossible to find. His quest is like the mind's search for control, order, and meaning in a world where everything is constantly disintegrating. The quest proves the futility of the quest. There is no way to overcome death; there is no way to control reality. "When I argue with reality, I lose," Byron Katie writes, "—but only 100 percent of the time."

Not until Gilgamesh gives up on transcendence can he realize how beautiful his city is; only then, freed from his restless heart, can he fully return to the place he started out from. Suppose that the city is this moment: things as they are, without any meaning added. When the mind gives up on its quest for control, order, and meaning, it finds that it has come home, to reality, where it has always been. What it has—what it is—in this very moment is everything it ever wanted.

Somehow, in the interval between story and return, Gilgamesh has become wise. He has absorbed not the conventional wisdom of a Shiduri or an Utnapishtim, but the deeper wisdom of the poem's narrative voice, a wisdom that is impartial, humorous, civilized, sexual, irreverent, skeptical of moral absolutes, delighted with the things of this world, and supremely confident in the power of its own language.

ABOUT THIS
VERSION

❀

I have called this a "version" of *Gilgamesh* rather than a translation. I don't read cuneiform and have no knowledge of Akkadian; for the meaning of the text, I have depended on literal translations by seven scholars. I am particularly indebted to A. R. George's superb, meticulous, monumental two-volume edition of the original texts, which far excels all previous scholarship. I have also read and profited from the translations of Jean Bottéro, Benjamin R. Foster, Maureen Gallery Kovacs, Albert Schott, and Raymond Jacques Tournay and Aaron Shaffer, as well as from the literary, nonscholarly versions of David Ferry and Raoul Schrott. Jean Bottéro's notes helped me in the interpretation of many passages.

My method was this: I first read and compared all the translations listed in the bibliography, understood the difficult passages to the best of my inexpert ability, and cobbled together a rough prose version. (Like many other translators, I have omitted Tablet XII, which most scholars consider as not belonging to the epic.) At this stage, I felt rather like a bat, feeling out the contours of the original text by flinging sound waves into the dark. Once my prose version was completed, I began the real work, of raising the language to the level of English verse. The line that I use, a loose, noniambic, nonalliterative tetrameter,* is rare in English; the two examples I know well are sections of Eliot's *Four Quartets* and Elizabeth Bishop's wonderful "Sestina." I worked hard to keep my rhythms from sounding too regular, and I varied them so that no two consecutive lines have the identical rhythm.

When possible, I kept fairly close to the literal meaning; when necessary, I was much freer and did not so much translate as adapt. I chose not to reproduce some of the quirks of Akkadian style, which for ancient readers may have been embellishments but are tedious for us: for example, the word-for-word repetitions of entire passages and the enumerations from one to seven or twelve. I filled in the many gaps in the text; I changed images that were unclear; I added lines when the drama of the situation called for elaboration or when passages ended abruptly and needed transitions; I cut out a number of fragmentary passages; and when the text was garbled, I occasionally changed the order of passages. (All these changes are documented in the notes.) While I have tried to be faithful to the spirit of the Akkadian text, I have often been as free with the letter of it as Sîn-lēqi-unninni and his Old Babylonian predecessors were with their material. I like to think that they would have approved.

---

* Except for the Prologue and the end of Book XI, which have five beats to the line.

GILGAMESH

He had seen everything, had experienced all emotions,
from exaltation to despair, had been granted a vision
into the great mystery, the secret places,
the primeval days before the Flood. He had journeyed
to the edge of the world and made his way back, exhausted
but whole. He had carved his trials on stone tablets,
had restored the holy Eanna Temple and the massive
wall of Uruk, which no city on earth can equal.
See how its ramparts gleam like copper in the sun.
Climb the stone staircase, more ancient than the mind can imagine,
approach the Eanna Temple, sacred to Ishtar,
a temple that no king has equaled in size or beauty,
walk on the wall of Uruk, follow its course
around the city, inspect its mighty foundations,
examine its brickwork, how masterfully it is built,

observe the land it encloses: the palm trees, the gardens,

the orchards, the glorious palaces and temples, the shops

and marketplaces, the houses, the public squares.

Find the cornerstone and under it the copper box

that is marked with his name. Unlock it. Open the lid.

Take out the tablet of lapis lazuli. Read

how Gilgamesh suffered all and accomplished all.

BOOK I

Surpassing all kings, powerful and tall

beyond all others, violent, splendid,

a wild bull of a man, unvanquished leader,

hero in the front lines, beloved by his soldiers—

fortress they called him, *protector of the people,*

raging flood that destroys all defenses—

two-thirds divine and one-third human,

son of King Lugalbanda, who became

a god, and of the goddess Ninsun,

he opened the mountain passes, dug wells

on the slopes, crossed the vast ocean, sailed

to the rising sun, journeyed to the edge

of the world, in search of eternal life,

and once he found Utnapishtim—the man

who survived the Great Flood and was made immortal—

he brought back the ancient, forgotten rites,

restoring the temples that the Flood had destroyed,

renewing the statutes and sacraments

for the welfare of the people and the sacred land.

Who is like Gilgamesh? What other king

has inspired such awe? Who else can say,

"I alone rule, supreme among mankind"?

The goddess Aruru, mother of creation,

had designed his body, had made him the strongest

of men—huge, handsome, radiant, perfect.

The city is his possession, he struts

through it, arrogant, his head raised high,

trampling its citizens like a wild bull.

He is king, he does whatever he wants,

takes the son from his father and crushes him,

takes the girl from her mother and uses her,

the warrior's daughter, the young man's bride,

he uses her, no one dares to oppose him.

But the people of Uruk cried out to heaven,

and their lamentation was heard, the gods

are not unfeeling, their hearts were touched,

they went to Anu, father of them all,

protector of the realm of sacred Uruk,

and spoke to him on the people's behalf:

"Heavenly Father, Gilgamesh—

noble as he is, splendid as he is—

has exceeded all bounds. The people suffer

from his tyranny, the people cry out

that he takes the son from his father and crushes him,

takes the girl from her mother and uses her,

the warrior's daughter, the young man's bride,

he uses her, no one dares to oppose him.

Is this how you want your king to rule?

Should a shepherd savage his own flock? Father,

do something, quickly, before the people

overwhelm heaven with their heartrending cries."

Anu heard them, he nodded his head,

then to the goddess, mother of creation,

he called out: "Aruru, you are the one

who created humans. Now go and create

a double for Gilgamesh, his second self,

a man who equals his strength and courage,

a man who equals his stormy heart.

Create a new hero, let them balance each other

perfectly, so that Uruk has peace."

When Aruru heard this, she closed her eyes,

and what Anu had commanded she formed in her mind.

She moistened her hands, she pinched off some clay,

she threw it into the wilderness,

kneaded it, shaped it to her idea,

and fashioned a man, a warrior, a hero:

Enkidu the brave, as powerful and fierce

as the war god Ninurta. Hair covered his body,

hair grew thick on his head and hung

down to his waist, like a woman's hair.

He roamed all over the wilderness,

naked, far from the cities of men,

ate grass with gazelles, and when he was thirsty

he drank clear water from the waterholes,

kneeling beside the antelope and deer.

One day, a human—a trapper—saw him

drinking with the animals at a waterhole.

The trapper's heart pounded, his face went white,

his legs shook, he was numb with terror.

The same thing happened a second, a third day.

Fear gripped his belly, he looked drained and haggard

like someone who has been on a long, hard journey.

He went to his father. "Father, I have seen

a savage man at the waterhole.

He must be the strongest man in the world,

with muscles like rock. I have seen him outrun

the swiftest animals. He lives among them,
eats grass with gazelles, and when he is thirsty
he drinks clear water from the waterholes.
I haven't approached him—I am too afraid.
He fills in the pits I have dug, he tears out
the traps I have set, he frees the animals,
and I can catch nothing. My livelihood is gone."

"Son, in Uruk there lives a man
named Gilgamesh. He is king of that city
and the strongest man in the world, they say,
with muscles like rock. Go now to Uruk,
go to Gilgamesh, tell him what happened,
then follow his advice. He will know what to do."

He made the journey, he stood before
Gilgamesh in the center of Uruk,
he told him about the savage man.
The king said, "Go to the temple of Ishtar,

ask them there for a woman named Shamhat,

one of the priestesses who give their bodies

to any man, in honor of the goddess.

Take her into the wilderness.

When the animals are drinking at the waterhole,

tell her to strip off her robe and lie there

naked, ready, with her legs apart.

The wild man will approach. Let her use her love-arts.

Nature will take its course, and then

the animals who knew him in the wilderness

will be bewildered, and will leave him forever."

The trapper found Shamhat, Ishtar's priestess,

and they went off into the wilderness.

For three days they walked. On the third day

they reached the waterhole. There they waited.

For two days they sat as the animals came

to drink clear water. Early in the morning

of the third day, Enkidu came and knelt down

to drink clear water with the antelope and deer.

They looked in amazement. The man was huge

and beautiful. Deep in Shamhat's loins

desire stirred. Her breath quickened

as she stared at this primordial being.

"Look," the trapper said, "there he is.

Now use your love-arts. Strip off your robe

and lie here naked, with your legs apart.

Stir up his lust when he approaches,

touch him, excite him, take his breath

with your kisses, show him what a woman is.

The animals who knew him in the wilderness

will be bewildered, and will leave him forever."

She stripped off her robe and lay there naked,

with her legs apart, touching herself.

Enkidu saw her and warily approached.

He sniffed the air. He gazed at her body.

He drew close, Shamhat touched him on the thigh,

touched his penis, and put him inside her.

She used her love-arts, she took his breath

with her kisses, held nothing back, and showed him

what a woman is. For seven days

he stayed erect and made love with her,

until he had had enough. At last

he stood up and walked toward the waterhole

to rejoin his animals. But the gazelles

saw him and scattered, the antelope and deer

bounded away. He tried to catch up,

but his body was exhausted, his life-force was spent,

his knees trembled, he could no longer run

like an animal, as he had before.

He turned back to Shamhat, and as he walked

he knew that his mind had somehow grown larger,

he knew things now that an animal can't know.

Enkidu sat down at Shamhat's feet.

He looked at her, and he understood

all the words she was speaking to him.
"Now, Enkidu, you know what it is
to be with a woman, to unite with her.
You are beautiful, you are like a god.
Why should you roam the wilderness
and live like an animal? Let me take you
to great-walled Uruk, to the temple of Ishtar,
to the palace of Gilgamesh the mighty king,
who in his arrogance oppresses the people,
trampling upon them like a wild bull."

She finished, and Enkidu nodded his head.
Deep in his heart he felt something stir,
a longing he had never known before,
the longing for a true friend. Enkidu said,
"I will go, Shamhat. Take me with you
to great-walled Uruk, to the temple of Ishtar,
to the palace of Gilgamesh the mighty king.
I will challenge him. I will shout to his face:

'*I* am the mightiest! *I* am the man

who can make the world tremble! *I* am supreme!' "

"Come," said Shamhat, "let us go to Uruk,

I will lead you to Gilgamesh the mighty king.

You will see the great city with its massive wall,

you will see the young men dressed in their splendor,

in the finest linen and embroidered wool,

brilliantly colored, with fringed shawls and wide belts.

Every day is a festival in Uruk,

with people singing and dancing in the streets,

musicians playing their lyres and drums,

the lovely priestesses standing before

the temple of Ishtar, chatting and laughing,

flushed with sexual joy, and ready

to serve men's pleasure, in honor of the goddess,

so that even old men are aroused from their beds.

You who are still so ignorant of life,

I will show you Gilgamesh the mighty king,

the hero destined for both joy and grief.

You will stand before him and gaze with wonder,

you will see how handsome, how virile he is,

how his body pulses with erotic power.

He is even taller and stronger than you—

so full of life-force that he needs no sleep.

Enkidu, put aside your aggression.

Shamash, the sun god, loves him, and his mind

has been made large by Anu, father of the gods,

made large by Enlil, the god of earth,

and by Ea, the god of water and wisdom.

Even before you came down from the hills,

you had come to Gilgamesh in a dream."

And she told Enkidu what she had heard.

"He went to his mother, the goddess Ninsun,

and asked her to interpret the dream.

'I saw a bright star, it shot across

the morning sky, it fell at my feet

and lay before me like a huge boulder.

I tried to lift it, but it was too heavy.

I tried to move it, but it would not budge.

A crowd of people gathered around me,

the people of Uruk pressed in to see it,

like a little baby they kissed its feet.

This boulder, this star that had fallen to earth—

I took it in my arms, I embraced and caressed it

the way a man caresses his wife.

Then I took it and laid it before you. You told me

that it was my double, my second self.'

The mother of Gilgamesh, Lady Ninsun,

the wise, the all-knowing, said to her son,

'Dearest child, this bright star from heaven,

this huge boulder that you could not lift—

it stands for a dear friend, a mighty hero.

You will take him in your arms, embrace and caress him

the way a man caresses his wife.

He will be your double, your second self,

a man who is loyal, who will stand at your side

through the greatest dangers. Soon you will meet him,

the companion of your heart. Your dream has said so.'

Gilgamesh said, 'May the dream come true.

May the true friend appear, the true companion,

who through every danger will stand at my side.' "

When Shamhat had finished speaking, Enkidu

turned to her, and again they made love.

BOOK II

Then Shamhat gave Enkidu one of her robes
and he put it on. Taking his hand,
she led him like a child to some shepherds' huts.

Marveling, the shepherds crowded around him.
"What an enormous man!" they whispered.
"How much like Gilgamesh he is—
tall and strong, with muscles like rock."
They led him to their table, they put bread and beer
in front of him. Enkidu sat and stared.
He had never seen human food, he didn't
know what to do. Then Shamhat said,
"Go ahead, Enkidu. This is food,
we humans eat and drink this." Warily
he tasted the bread. Then he ate a piece,

he ate a whole loaf, then ate another,

he ate until he was full, drank seven

pitchers of the beer, his heart grew light,

his face glowed, and he sang out with joy.

He had his hair cut, he washed, he rubbed

sweet oil into his skin, and became

fully human. Shining, he looked

handsome as a bridegroom. When the shepherds lay down,

Enkidu went out with sword and spear.

He chased off lions and wolves, all night

he guarded the flocks, he stayed awake

and guarded them while the shepherds slept.

One day, while he was making love,

he looked up and saw a young man pass by.

"Shamhat," he said, "bring that man here.

I want to talk to him. Where is he going?"

She called out, then went to the man and said,

"Where are you going in such a rush?"

The man said to Enkidu, "I am on my way
to a wedding banquet. I have piled the table
with exquisite food for the ceremony.
The priest will bless the young couple, the guests
will rejoice, the bridegroom will step aside,
and the virgin will wait in the marriage bed
for Gilgamesh, king of great-walled Uruk.
It is he who mates first with the lawful wife.
After he is done, the bridegroom follows.
This is the order that the gods have decreed.
From the moment the king's birth-cord was cut,
every girl's hymen has belonged to him."

As he listened, Enkidu's face went pale
with anger. "I will go to Uruk now,
to the palace of Gilgamesh the mighty king.
I will challenge him. I will shout to his face:
'*I* am the mightiest! *I* am the man
who can make the world tremble! *I* am supreme!'"

Together they went to great-walled Uruk,

Enkidu in front, Shamhat behind him.

When he walked into the main street of Uruk,

the people gathered around him, marveling,

the crowds kept pressing closer to see him,

like a little baby they kissed his feet.

"What an enormous man!" they whispered.

"How much like Gilgamesh—not quite so tall

but stronger-boned. In the wilderness

he grew up eating grass with gazelles,

he was nursed on the milk of antelope and deer.

Gilgamesh truly has met his match.

This wild man can rival the mightiest of kings."

The wedding ritual had taken place,

the musicians were playing their drums and lyres,

the guests were eating, singing and laughing,

the bride was ready for Gilgamesh

as though for a god, she was waiting in her bed

to open to him, in honor of Ishtar,

to forget her husband and open to the king.

When Gilgamesh reached the marriage house,

Enkidu was there. He stood like a boulder,

blocking the door. Gilgamesh, raging,

stepped up and seized him, huge arms gripped

huge arms, foreheads crashed like wild bulls,

the two men staggered, they pitched against houses,

the doorposts trembled, the outer walls shook,

they careened through the streets, they grappled each other,

limbs intertwined, each huge body

straining to break free from the other's embrace.

Finally, Gilgamesh threw the wild man

and with his right knee pinned him to the ground.

His anger left him. He turned away.

The contest was over. Enkidu said,

"Gilgamesh, you are unique among humans.

Your mother, the goddess Ninsun, made you

stronger and braver than any mortal,

and rightly has Enlil granted you the kingship,

since you are destined to rule over men."

They embraced and kissed. They held hands like brothers.

They walked side by side. They became true friends.

BOOK III

Time passed quickly. Gilgamesh said,
"Now we must travel to the Cedar Forest,
where the fierce monster Humbaba lives.
We must kill him and drive out evil from the world."

Enkidu sighed. His eyes filled with tears.
Gilgamesh said, "Why are you sighing?
Why, dear friend, do your eyes fill with tears?"

Enkidu answered, "Dear friend, a scream
sticks in my throat, my arms are limp.
I knew that country when I roamed the hills
with the antelope and deer. The forest is endless,
it spreads far and wide for a thousand miles.
What man would dare to penetrate its depths?"

Gilgamesh said, "Listen, dear friend,

even if the forest goes on forever,

I have to enter it, climb its slopes,

cut down a cedar that is tall enough

to make a whirlwind as it falls to earth."

Enkidu said, "But how can any man

dare to enter the Cedar Forest?

It is sacred to Enlil. Hasn't he declared

its entrance forbidden, hasn't he put

Humbaba there to terrify men?

We must not go on this journey, we must not

fight this creature. His breath spews fire,

his voice booms like thunder, his jaws are death.

He can hear all sounds in the forest, even

the faintest rustling among the leaves,

he will hear us a hundred miles away.

Who among men or gods could defeat him?

Humbaba is the forest's guardian, Enlil

put him there to terrify men.

Whoever enters will be struck down by fear."

Gilgamesh answered, "Why, dear friend,

do you speak like a coward? What you just said

is unworthy of you, it grieves my heart.

We are not gods, we cannot ascend

to heaven. No, we are mortal men.

Only the gods live forever. *Our* days

are few in number, and whatever we achieve

is a puff of wind. Why be afraid then,

since sooner or later death must come?

Where is the courage you have always had?

If I die in the forest on this great adventure,

won't you be ashamed when people say,

'Gilgamesh met a hero's death

battling the monster Humbaba. And where

was Enkidu? He was safe at home!'

You were raised in the mountains, with your own hands

you have killed marauding lions and wolves,

you are brave, your heart has been tested in combat.

But whether you come along or not,

I will cut down the tree, I will kill Humbaba,

I will make a lasting name for myself,

I will stamp my fame on men's minds forever."

Gilgamesh bolted the seven gates

of great-walled Uruk, and the people gathered,

crowds of them poured out into the streets.

Gilgamesh sat on his throne. The crowds

pressed in to hear him. Gilgamesh spoke:

"Hear me, elders of great-walled Uruk.

I must travel now to the Cedar Forest,

where the fierce monster Humbaba lives.

I will conquer him in the Cedar Forest,

I will cut down the tree, I will kill Humbaba,

the whole world will know how mighty I am.

I will make a lasting name for myself,

I will stamp my fame on men's minds forever."

Then Gilgamesh turned to the young men and spoke:

"Hear me, young men of great-walled Uruk,

warriors and comrades who have fought at my side.

I will journey to meet the monster Humbaba,

I will walk a road that no man has traveled,

I will face a combat that no man has known.

Give me your blessing before I leave,

so that I may come back from the Cedar Forest

victorious, and see your faces again.

Once again may I celebrate the New Year

with you, in the streets of great-walled Uruk,

to the lyre's sound and the beat of the drums."

Enkidu stood up. There were tears in his eyes.

"Elders of Uruk, persuade the king

not to go to the Cedar Forest,

not to fight the fierce monster Humbaba,

whose roar booms forth like a thunderclap,

whose breath spews fire, whose jaws are death,

who can hear all sounds in the forest, even

the faintest rustling among the leaves.

Who among men or gods could defeat him?

Humbaba is the forest's guardian, Enlil

put him there to terrify men."

The elders bowed to the king and said,

"You are young, Sire, your heart beats high

and runs away with you. Why do you wish

to embark on this folly? We have heard of Humbaba,

he is dangerous, he is horrible to look at,

his breath spews fire, his jaws are death.

How can any man, even you,

dare to enter the Cedar Forest?

Who among men or gods could defeat him?

Humbaba is the forest's guardian, Enlil

put him there to terrify men."

After he had listened to the elders' words,

Gilgamesh laughed. He got up and said,

"Dear friend, tell me, has your courage returned?

Are you ready to leave? Or are you still

afraid of dying a hero's death?

Enkidu, let us go to the forge

and order the smiths to make us weapons

that only the mightiest heroes could use."

Enkidu listened gravely. He stood

silent there for a long time. At last

he nodded. Gilgamesh took his hand.

The smiths listened to their instructions.

They cast huge weapons that ordinary men

could never carry: axes that weighed

two hundred pounds each, knives with cross guards

and heavy mountings of solid gold.

Each man carried weapons and armor

weighing more than six hundred pounds.

Gilgamesh said, "Before we leave,

let us pay a visit to my mother's temple,

let us go and speak to the lady Ninsun,

the wise, the all-knowing. Let us bow before her,

let us ask for her blessing and her advice."

Hand in hand, the two friends walked

to Ninsun's temple. Gilgamesh bowed

to his mother, the goddess Ninsun, and said,

"I must travel now to the Cedar Forest,

I must journey to meet the fierce monster Humbaba,

I must walk a road that no man has traveled,

I must face a combat that no man has known.

Dear mother, great goddess, help me in this,

give me your blessing before I leave,

so that I may come back from the Cedar Forest

victorious, and see your face again."

Ninsun listened to his words with sorrow.

With sorrow she entered her inner room,

she bathed in water of tamarisk and soapwort,

she put on her finest robe, a wide belt,

a jeweled necklace, then put on her crown.

She climbed the stairs and went up to the roof,

she lit sweet incense in honor of Shamash,

she lifted her arms in prayer and said,

"Lord of heaven, you have granted my son

beauty and strength and courage—why

have you burdened him with a restless heart?

Now you have stirred him up to attack

the monster Humbaba, to make a long

journey from which he may not return.

Since he has resolved to go, protect him

until he arrives at the Cedar Forest,

until he kills the monster Humbaba

and drives from the world the evil that you hate.

Protect him each day as you cross the sky,

and at twilight may Aya your bride entrust him

to the valiant stars, the watchmen of the night.

O Lord Shamash, glorious sun,

delight of the gods, illuminator

of the world, who rise and the light is born,

it fills the heavens, the whole earth takes shape,

the mountains form, the valleys grow bright,

darkness vanishes, evil retreats,

all creatures wake up and open their eyes,

they see you, they are filled with joy—

protect my son. On his dangerous journey

let the days be long, let the nights be short,

let his stride be vigorous and his legs sturdy.

When he and his dear friend Enkidu arrive,

stir up strong winds against Humbaba,

the south wind, the north wind, the east and the west,

storm wind, gale wind, hurricane, tornado,

to pin Humbaba, to paralyze his steps

and make it easy for my son to kill him.

Then your swift mules will carry you onward

to your stopping place and bed for the night,

the gods will bring luscious food to delight you,

Aya will dry your face with the fringe

of her pure white robe. Hear me, O Lord,

protect my son, in your great mercy

lead him to the Forest, then bring him home."

After she had prayed, the goddess Ninsun,

the wise, the all-knowing, came down from the roof

and summoned Enkidu. "Dear child," she said,

"you were not born from my womb, but now

I adopt you as my son." She hung a jeweled

amulet around Enkidu's neck.

"As a priestess takes in an abandoned child,

I have taken in Enkidu as my own son.

May he be a brother for Gilgamesh.

May he guide him to the Forest, and bring him home."

Enkidu listened. Tears filled his eyes.

He and Gilgamesh clasped hands like brothers.

They took their weapons: the massive axes,

the massive knives, the quivers, the bows.

The elders made way. The young men cheered.

The elders stood up and addressed the king:

"Come back safely to great-walled Uruk.

Do not rely on your strength alone,

but be watchful, be wary, make each blow count.

Remember what the ancient proverb says:

'If you walk in front, you protect your comrade;

if you know the route, you safeguard your friend.'

Let Enkidu go ahead as you walk,

he knows the way to the Cedar Forest,

he is tested in battle, he is brave and strong,

he will guard you at every stage of the journey,

through every danger he will stand at your side.

May Shamash grant you your heart's desire,

may the path to the Cedar Forest be straight,

may the nights be safe, with no dangers lurking,

may your father Lugalbanda protect you,

may you conquer Humbaba, may the battle be quick,

may you joyfully wash your feet in his river.

Dig a well when you stop for the night,

fill your waterskins with fresh water,

each day make an offering to Shamash,

and remember Lugalbanda your father,

who journeyed to far-off mountains himself."

The elders turned to Enkidu and said,

"We leave the king in your care. Protect him,

guide him through all the treacherous passes,

show him where to find food and where

to dig for fresh water, lead him to the Forest

and fight at his side. May Shamash help you,

may the gods grant you your heart's desire

and bring you back safe to great-walled Uruk."

Enkidu said to Gilgamesh,

"Since you must do this, I must go with you.

So let us leave. Let our hearts be fearless.

I will go first, since I know the way

to the Cedar Forest, where Humbaba lives."

BOOK IV

At four hundred miles they stopped to eat,
at a thousand miles they pitched their camp.
They had traveled for just three days and nights,
a six weeks' journey for ordinary men.
When the sun was setting, they dug a well,
they filled their waterskins with fresh water,
Gilgamesh climbed to the mountaintop,
he poured out flour as an offering and said,
"Mountain, bring me a favorable dream."
Enkidu did the ritual for dreams,
praying for a sign. A gust of wind
passed. He built a shelter for the night,
placed Gilgamesh on the floor and spread
a magic circle of flour around him,

then sprawled like a net across the doorway.

Gilgamesh sat there, with his chin on his knees,

and sleep overcame him, as it does all men.

At midnight he awoke. He said to Enkidu,

"What happened? Did you touch me? Did a god pass by?

What makes my skin creep? Why am I cold?

Enkidu, dear friend, I have had a dream,

a horrible dream. We were walking in a gorge,

and when I looked up, a huge mountain loomed,

so huge that we were as small as flies.

Then the mountain fell down on top of us.

Dear friend, tell me, what does this mean?"

Enkidu said, "Don't worry, my friend,

the dream you had is a favorable one.

The mountain stands for Humbaba. He will fall

just like that mountain. Lord Shamash will grant us

victory, we will kill the monster

and leave his corpse on the battlefield."
Gilgamesh, happy with his good dream,
smiled, and his face lit up with pleasure.

At four hundred miles they stopped to eat,
at a thousand miles they pitched their camp.
They had traveled for just three days and nights,
a six weeks' journey for ordinary men.
When the sun was setting, they dug a well,
they filled their waterskins with fresh water,
Gilgamesh climbed to the mountaintop,
he poured out flour as an offering and said,
"Mountain, bring me a favorable dream."
Enkidu did the ritual for dreams,
praying for a sign. A gust of wind
passed. He built a shelter for the night,
placed Gilgamesh on the floor and spread
a magic circle of flour around him,
then sprawled like a net across the doorway.

Gilgamesh sat there, with his chin on his knees,

and sleep overcame him, as it does all men.

At midnight he awoke. He said to Enkidu,

"What happened? Did you touch me? Did a god pass by?

What makes my skin creep? Why am I cold?

Enkidu, dear friend, I have had a dream,

a dream more horrible than the first.

I looked up and a huge mountain loomed,

it threw me down, it pinned me by the feet,

a terrifying brightness hurt my eyes,

suddenly a young man appeared,

he was shining and handsome, he took me by the arm,

he pulled me out from under the mountain,

he gave me water, my heart grew calm.

Dear friend, tell me, what does this mean?"

Enkidu said, "Don't worry, my friend,

the dream you had is a favorable one.

Again, the mountain stands for Humbaba.

He threw you down, but he could not kill you.

As for the handsome young man who appeared,

he stands for Lord Shamash, who will rescue you

and grant you everything you desire."

Gilgamesh, happy with his good dream,

smiled, and his face lit up with pleasure.

At four hundred miles they stopped to eat,

at a thousand miles they pitched their camp.

They had traveled for just three days and nights,

a six weeks' journey for ordinary men.

When the sun was setting, they dug a well,

they filled their waterskins with fresh water,

Gilgamesh climbed to the mountaintop,

he poured out flour as an offering and said,

"Mountain, bring me a favorable dream."

Enkidu did the ritual for dreams,

praying for a sign. A gust of wind

passed. He built a shelter for the night,
placed Gilgamesh on the floor and spread
a magic circle of flour around him,
then sprawled like a net across the doorway.
Gilgamesh sat there, with his chin on his knees,
and sleep overcame him, as it does all men.

At midnight he awoke. He said to Enkidu,
"What happened? Did you touch me? Did a god pass by?
What makes my skin creep? Why am I cold?
Enkidu, dear friend, I have had a dream,
a dream more horrible than both the others.
The heavens roared and the earth heaved,
then darkness, silence. Lightning flashed,
igniting the trees. By the time the flames
died out, the ground was covered with ash.
Dear friend, tell me, what does this mean?"

Enkidu said, "Don't worry, my friend,

the dream you had is a favorable one.

The fiery heavens stand for Humbaba,

who tried to kill you with lightning and flames.

But in spite of the fire, he could not harm you.

We will kill Humbaba. Success is ours.

However he attacks us, we will prevail."

Gilgamesh, happy with his good dream,

smiled, and his face lit up with pleasure.

At four hundred miles they stopped to eat,

at a thousand miles they pitched their camp.

They had traveled for just three days and nights,

a six weeks' journey for ordinary men.

When the sun was setting, they dug a well,

they filled their waterskins with fresh water,

Gilgamesh climbed to the mountaintop,

he poured out flour as an offering and said,

"Mountain, bring me a favorable dream."
Enkidu did the ritual for dreams,
praying for a sign. A gust of wind
passed. He built a shelter for the night,
placed Gilgamesh on the floor and spread
a magic circle of flour around him,
then sprawled like a net across the doorway.
Gilgamesh sat there, with his chin on his knees,
and sleep overcame him, as it does all men.

At midnight he awoke. He said to Enkidu,
"What happened? Did you touch me? Did a god pass by?
What makes my skin creep? Why am I cold?
Enkidu, dear friend, I have had a fourth dream,
a dream more horrible than the three others.
I saw a fierce eagle with a lion's head,
it floated down toward me like a huge cloud,
it grimaced at me, terrifying flames
shot from its mouth, then beside me I saw

a young man with an unearthly glow,

he seized the creature, he broke its wings,

he wrung its neck and threw it to the ground.

Dear friend, tell me, what does this mean?"

Enkidu said, "Don't worry, my friend,

the dream you had is a favorable one.

The eagle that you saw, with a lion's head,

stands for Humbaba. Though it dived straight toward you

and terrifying flames shot from its mouth,

nothing could cause you harm. The young man

who came to your rescue was our lord, Shamash.

He will stand beside us when the monster attacks.

Whatever happens, we will prevail."

Gilgamesh, happy with his good dream,

smiled, and his face lit up with pleasure.

At four hundred miles they stopped to eat,

at a thousand miles they pitched their camp.

They had traveled for just three days and nights,

a six weeks' journey for ordinary men.

When the sun was setting, they dug a well,

they filled their waterskins with fresh water,

Gilgamesh climbed to the mountaintop,

he poured out flour as an offering and said,

"Mountain, bring me a favorable dream."

Enkidu did the ritual for dreams,

praying for a sign. A gust of wind

passed. He built a shelter for the night,

placed Gilgamesh on the floor and spread

a magic circle of flour around him,

then sprawled like a net across the doorway.

Gilgamesh sat there, with his chin on his knees,

and sleep overcame him, as it does all men.

At midnight he awoke. He said to Enkidu,

"What happened? Did you touch me? Did a god pass by?

What makes my skin creep? Why am I cold?

Enkidu, dear friend, I have had a fifth dream,

a dream more horrible than all the others.

I was wrestling with a gigantic bull,

its bellow shattered the ground and raised

clouds of dust that darkened the sky,

it pinned me down, it crushed me, I felt

its breath on my face, then suddenly a man

pulled me up, put his arms around me,

and gave me fresh water from his waterskin.

Dear friend, tell me, what does this mean?"

Enkidu said, "Don't worry, my friend,

the dream you had is a favorable one.

The gigantic bull is no enemy of ours.

He stands for the very god who has helped us,

bright Shamash, our protector, lord of the sky,

who in every danger will come to our aid.

The man who pulled you up from the ground
and gave you fresh water from his waterskin
is Lugalbanda, your personal god.
With *his* help, we will achieve a triumph
greater than any man has achieved."

They had reached the edge of the Cedar Forest.
They could hear Humbaba's terrifying roar.
Gilgamesh stopped. He was trembling. Tears
flowed down his cheeks. "O Shamash," he cried,
"protect me on this dangerous journey.
Remember me, help me, hear my prayer."
They stood and listened. A moment passed.
Then, from heaven, the voice of the god
called to Gilgamesh: "Hurry, attack,
attack Humbaba while the time is right,
before he enters the depths of the forest,
before he can hide there and wrap himself

in his seven auras with their paralyzing glare.

He is wearing just one now. Attack him! Now!"

They stood at the edge of the Cedar Forest,

gazing, silent. There was nothing to say.

BOOK V

They stood at the edge of the Cedar Forest,
marveling at the great height of the trees.
They could see, before them, a well-marked trail
beaten by Humbaba as he came and went.
From far off they saw the Cedar Mountain,
sacred to Ishtar, where the gods dwell,
the slopes of it steep, and rich in cedars
with their sharp fragrance and pleasant shade.
Gripping their axes, their knives unsheathed,
they entered the Forest and made their way through
the tangle of thorn bushes underfoot.

Suddenly Enkidu was seized by terror,
his face turned pale like a severed head.
He said to Gilgamesh, "Dear friend, I cannot

continue, I am frightened, I cannot go on.

You go into the dreadful forest,

you kill Humbaba and win the fame.

I will return now to great-walled Uruk,

and all men will know what a coward I have been."

Gilgamesh answered, "Dear friend, dear brother,

I cannot kill Humbaba alone.

Please stay here with me. Stand at my side.

'Two boats lashed together will never sink.

A three-ply rope is not easily broken.'

If we help each other and fight side by side,

what harm can come to us? Let us go on

and attack the monster. We have come so far.

Whatever you are feeling, let us go on."

Enkidu said, "You have never met him,

so you don't know the horror that lurks ahead.

But when I saw him, my blood ran cold.

His teeth are knife-sharp, they stick out like tusks,

his face, blood-smeared, is a lion's face,

he charges ahead like a raging torrent,

his forehead ablaze. Who can withstand him?

I am terrified. I cannot go on."

Gilgamesh said, "Courage, dear brother,

this is no time to give in to fear.

We have come so far, across so many mountains,

and our journey is about to reach its goal.

You were raised in the wild, with your own hands

you have killed marauding lions and wolves,

you are brave, your heart has been tested in combat.

Though your arms feel weak now and your legs tremble,

you are a warrior, you know what to do.

Shout out your battle-cry, let your voice pound

like a kettle drum. Let your heart inspire you

to be joyous in battle, to forget about death.

If we help each other and fight side by side,

we will make a lasting name for ourselves,
we will stamp our fame on men's minds forever."

They walked deep into the Cedar Forest,
gripping their axes, their knives unsheathed,
following the trail that Humbaba had made.

They came within sight of the monster's den.
He was waiting inside it. Their blood ran cold.
He saw the two friends, he grimaced, he bared
his teeth, he let out a deafening roar.
He glared at Gilgamesh. "Young man," he said,
"you will never go home. Prepare to die."
Dread surged through Gilgamesh, terror flooded
his muscles, his heart froze, his mouth went dry,
his legs shook, his feet were rooted to the ground.

Enkidu saw his dismay and said,
"Dear friend, great warrior, noble hero,

don't lose courage, remember this:

'Two boats lashed together will never sink.

A three-ply rope is not easily broken.'

If we help each other and fight side by side,

what harm can come to us? Let us go on."

They advanced to the monster's den. Humbaba

charged out roaring at them and said,

"I know you, Gilgamesh. Don't be a fool.

Go away. Leave the Cedar Forest.

Have madmen told you to confront me here?

I will tear you limb from limb, I will crush you

and leave you bloody and mangled on the ground.

And you, Enkidu, you son of a fish

or a turtle, you gutless, fatherless spawn

who never suckled on mother's milk,

I saw you in the pastures when you were young,

I saw you graze with the wandering herds

but I didn't kill you, you were too scrawny,

you wouldn't have made a decent meal.

And now you dare to lead Gilgamesh here,

you both stand before me looking like a pair

of frightened girls. I will slit your throats,

I will cut off your heads, I will feed your stinking

guts to the shrieking vultures and crows."

Gilgamesh backed away. He said,

"How dreadful Humbaba's face has become!

It is changing into a thousand nightmare

faces, more horrible than I can bear.

I feel haunted. I am too afraid to go on."

Enkidu answered, "Why, dear friend,

do you speak like a coward? What you just said

is unworthy of you. It grieves my heart.

We must not hesitate or retreat.

Two intimate friends cannot be defeated.

Be courageous. Remember how strong you are.

I will stand by you. Now let us attack."

Gilgamesh felt his courage return.

They charged at Humbaba like two wild bulls.

The monster let out a deafening cry,

his roar boomed forth like a blast of thunder,

he stamped and the ground burst open, his steps

split the mountains of Lebanon,

the clouds turned black, a sulfurous fog

descended on them and made their eyes ache.

Then Shamash threw strong winds at Humbaba,

the south wind, the north wind, the east and the west,

storm wind, gale wind, hurricane, tornado,

to pin him down and paralyze his steps.

He could not move forward, could not retreat.

Gilgamesh saw it, he leaped upon him,

he held a knife to Humbaba's throat.

❀

Humbaba said, "Gilgamesh, have mercy.

Let me live here in the Cedar Forest.

If you spare my life, I will be your slave,

I will give you as many cedars as you wish.

You are king of Uruk by the grace of Shamash,

honor him with a cedar temple

and a glorious cedar palace for yourself.

All this is yours, if only you spare me."

Enkidu said, "Dear friend, don't listen

to anything that the monster says.

Kill him before you become confused."

Humbaba said, "If any mortal,

Enkidu, knows the rules of my forest,

it is you. You know that this is my place

and that I am the forest's guardian. Enlil

put me here to terrify men,

and I guard the forest as Enlil ordains.

If you kill me, you will call down the gods'

wrath, and their judgment will be severe.

I could have killed *you* at the forest's edge,

I could have hung you from a cedar and fed

your guts to the shrieking vultures and crows.

Now it is your turn to show me mercy.

Speak to him, beg him to spare my life."

Enkidu said, "Dear friend, quickly,

before another moment goes by,

kill Humbaba, don't listen to his words,

don't hesitate, slaughter him, slit his throat,

before the great god Enlil can stop us,

before the great gods can get enraged,

Enlil in Nippur, Shamash in Larsa.

Establish your fame, so that forever

men will speak of brave Gilgamesh,

who killed Humbaba in the Cedar Forest."

Knowing he was doomed, Humbaba cried out,

"I curse you both. Because you have done this,

may Enkidu die, may he die in great pain,

may Gilgamesh be inconsolable,

may his merciless heart be crushed with grief."

Gilgamesh dropped his axe, appalled.

Enkidu said, "Courage, dear friend.

Close your ears to Humbaba's curses.

Don't listen to a word. Slaughter him! Now!"

Gilgamesh, hearing his beloved friend,

came to himself. He yelled, he lifted

his massive axe, he swung it, it tore

into Humbaba's neck, the blood

shot out, again the axe bit flesh

and bone, the monster staggered, his eyes

rolled, and at the axe's third stroke

he toppled like a cedar and crashed to the ground.

At his death-roar the mountains of Lebanon shook,

the valleys ran with his blood, for ten miles

the forest resounded. Then the two friends

sliced him open, pulled out his intestines,

cut off his head with its knife-sharp teeth

and horrible bloodshot staring eyes.

A gentle rain fell onto the mountains.

A gentle rain fell onto the mountains.

They took their axes and penetrated

deeper into the forest, they went

chopping down cedars, the woods chips flew,

Gilgamesh chopped down the mighty trees,

Enkidu hewed the trunks into timbers.

Enkidu said, "By your great strength

you have killed Humbaba, the forest's watchman.

What could bring you dishonor now?

We have chopped down the trees of the Cedar Forest,

we have brought to earth the highest of the trees,

the cedar whose top once pierced the sky.

We will make it into a gigantic door,

a hundred feet high and thirty feet wide,

we will float it down the Euphrates to Enlil's

temple in Nippur. No men shall go through it,

but only the gods. May Enlil delight in it,

may it be a joy to the people of Nippur."

They bound logs together and built a raft.

Enkidu steered it down the great river.

Gilgamesh carried Humbaba's head.

BOOK VI

When he returned to great-walled Uruk,
Gilgamesh bathed, he washed his matted
hair and shook it over his back,
he took off his filthy, blood-spattered clothes,
put on a tunic of the finest wool,
wrapped himself in a glorious gold-trimmed
purple robe and fastened it with
a wide fringed belt, then put on his crown.

The goddess Ishtar caught sight of him,
she saw how splendid a man he was,
her heart was smitten, her loins caught fire.

"Come here, Gilgamesh," Ishtar said,
"marry me, give me your luscious fruits,

be my husband, be my sweet man.

I will give you abundance beyond your dreams:

marble and alabaster, ivory and jade,

gorgeous servants with blue-green eyes,

a chariot of lapis lazuli

with golden wheels and guide-horns of amber,

pulled by storm-demons like giant mules.

When you enter my temple and its cedar fragrance,

high priests will bow down and kiss your feet,

kings and princes will kneel before you,

bringing you tribute from east and west.

And I will bless everything that you own,

your goats will bear triplets, your ewes will twin,

your donkeys will be faster than any mule,

your chariot-horses will win every race,

your oxen will be the envy of the world.

These are the least of the gifts I will shower

upon you. Come here. Be my sweet man."

Gilgamesh said, "Your price is too high,

such riches are far beyond my means.

Tell me, how could I ever repay you,

even if I gave you jewels, perfumes,

rich robes? And what will happen to me

when your heart turns elsewhere and your lust burns out?

"Why would I want to be the lover

of a broken oven that fails in the cold,

a flimsy door that the wind blows through,

a palace that falls on its staunchest defenders,

a mouse that gnaws through its thin reed shelter,

tar that blackens the workman's hands,

a waterskin that is full of holes

and leaks all over its bearer, a piece

of limestone that crumbles and undermines

a solid stone wall, a battering ram

that knocks down the rampart of an allied city,

a shoe that mangles its owner's foot?

"Which of your husbands did you love forever?
Which could satisfy your endless desires?
Let me remind you of how they suffered,
how each one came to a bitter end.
Remember what happened to that beautiful boy
Tammuz: you loved him when you were both young,
then you changed, you sent him to the underworld
and doomed him to be wailed for, year after year.
You loved the bright-speckled roller bird,
then you changed, you attacked him and broke his wings,
and he sits in the woods crying *Ow-ee! Ow-ee!*
You loved the lion, matchless in strength,
then you changed, you dug seven pits for him,
and when he fell, you left him to die.
You loved the hot-blooded, war-bold stallion,
then you changed, you doomed him to whip and spurs,
to endlessly gallop, with a bit in his mouth,
to muddy his own water when he drinks from a pool,

and for his mother, the goddess Silili,

you ordained a weeping that will never end.

You loved the shepherd, the master of the flocks,

who every day would bake bread for you

and would bring you a fresh-slaughtered, roasted lamb,

then you changed, you touched him, he became a wolf,

and now his own shepherd boys drive him away

and his own dogs snap at his hairy thighs.

You loved the gardener Ishullanu,

who would bring you baskets of fresh-picked dates,

every day, to brighten your table,

you lusted for him, you drew close and said,

'Sweet Ishullanu, let me suck your rod,

touch my vagina, caress my jewel,'

and he frowned and answered, 'Why should I eat

this rotten meal of yours? What can you offer

but the bread of dishonor, the beer of shame,

and thin reeds as covers when the cold wind blows?'

But you kept up your sweet-talk and at last he gave in,

then you changed, you turned him into a toad
and doomed him to live in his devastated garden.
And why would *my* fate be any different?
If I too became your lover, you would treat me
as cruelly as you treated them."

Ishtar shrieked, she exploded with fury.
Raging, weeping, she went up to heaven,
to her father, Anu, and Antu, her mother,
as tears of anger poured down her cheeks.
"Father, Gilgamesh slandered me!
He hurled the worst insults at me, he said
horrible, unforgivable things!"

Anu said to the princess Ishtar,
"But might you not have provoked this? Did you
try to seduce him? Or did he just start
insulting you for no reason at all?"

Ishtar said, "Please, Father, I beg you,
give me the Bull of Heaven, just
for a little while. I want to bring it
to the earth, I want it to kill that liar
Gilgamesh and destroy his palace.
If you say no, I will smash the gates
of the underworld, and a million famished
ghouls will ascend to devour the living,
and the living will be outnumbered by the dead."

Anu said to the princess Ishtar,
"But if I give you the Bull of Heaven,
Uruk will have famine for seven long years.
Have you provided the people with grain
for seven years, and the cattle with fodder?"

Ishtar said, "Yes, of course I have gathered
grain and fodder, I have stored up enough—
more than enough—for seven years."

When Anu heard this, he called for the Bull

and handed its nose rope to the princess Ishtar.

Ishtar led the Bull down to the earth,

it entered and bellowed, the whole land shook,

the streams and marshes dried up, the Euphrates'

water level dropped by ten feet.

When the Bull snorted, the earth cracked open

and a hundred warriors fell in and died.

It snorted again, the earth cracked open

and two hundred warriors fell in and died.

When it snorted a third time, the earth cracked open

and Enkidu fell in, up to his waist,

he jumped out and grabbed the Bull's horns, it spat

its slobber into his face, it lifted

its tail and spewed dung all over him.

Gilgamesh rushed in and shouted, "Dear friend,

keep fighting, together we are sure to win."

Enkidu circled behind the Bull,

seized it by the tail and set his foot

on its haunch, then Gilgamesh skillfully,

like a butcher, strode up and thrust his knife

between its shoulders and the base of its horns.

After they had killed the Bull of Heaven,

they ripped out its heart and they offered it

to Shamash. Then they both bowed before him

and sat down like brothers, side by side.

Ishtar was outraged. She climbed to the top

of Uruk's great wall, she writhed in grief

and wailed, "Not only did Gilgamesh

slander me—now the brute has killed

his own punishment, the Bull of Heaven."

When Enkidu heard these words, he laughed,

he reached down, ripped off one of the Bull's

thighs, and flung it in Ishtar's face.

"If only I could catch you, this is what
I would do to you, I would rip *you* apart
and drape the Bull's guts over your arms!"

Ishtar assembled her priestesses,
those who offer themselves to all men
in her honor. They placed the Bull's gory thigh
on the altar, and began a solemn lament.

Gilgamesh summoned his master craftsmen.
They marveled at the gigantic horns.
Each horn was made from thirty pounds
of lapis lazuli, each was as thick
as the length of two thumbs, together they held
four hundred gallons. He called for that much
oil to anoint his father's statue,
then hung the two massive horns in the chapel
dedicated to Lugalbanda.

The two friends washed themselves in the river

and returned to the palace, hand in hand.

They rode in a chariot through the main streets,

the people shouted and cheered as they passed.

Gilgamesh said to his singing girls,

"Tell me: Who is the handsomest of men?

Tell me: Who is the bravest of heroes?

Gilgamesh—he is the handsomest of men,

Enkidu—he is the bravest of heroes.

We are the victors who in our fury

flung the Bull's thigh in Ishtar's face,

and now, in the streets, she has no one to avenge her."

There was singing and feasting in the palace that night.

Later, when the warriors were stretched out asleep,

Enkidu had a terrifying dream.

When he woke up, he said to Gilgamesh,

"Dear friend, why are the great gods assembled?"

BOOK VII

"Beloved brother," Enkidu said,
"last night I had a terrifying dream.
I dreamed that we had offended the gods,
they met in council and Anu said,
'They have slaughtered the Bull of Heaven and killed
Humbaba, watchman of the Cedar Forest.
Therefore one of the two must die.'
Then Enlil said to him, 'Enkidu,
not Gilgamesh, is the one who must die.' "

Enkidu fell sick. He lay on his bed,
sick at heart, and his tears flowed like streams.
He said to Gilgamesh, "Dear friend, dear brother,
they are taking me from you. I will not return.

I will sit with the dead in the underworld,

and never will I see my dear brother again."

When Gilgamesh heard his friend's words, he wept,

swiftly the tears flowed down his cheeks.

He said to Enkidu, "Dearest brother,

you have been a reasonable man, but now

you are talking nonsense. How do you know

that your dream is not a favorable one?

Fear has set your lips buzzing like flies."

Enkidu said, "Beloved brother,

last night I had a second bad dream.

The heavens thundered, the earth replied,

and I was standing on a shadowy plain.

A creature appeared with a lion's head,

his face was ghastly, he had a lion's

paws, an eagle's talons and wings.

He flew at me, he seized me by the hair,

I tried to struggle, but with one blow

he capsized me like a raft, he leaped

upon me, like a bull he trampled my bones.

'Gilgamesh, save me, save me!' I cried.

But you didn't save me. You were afraid

and you didn't come. The creature touched me

and suddenly feathers covered my arms,

he bound them behind me and forced me down

to the underworld, the house of darkness,

the home of the dead, where all who enter

never return to the sweet earth again.

Those who dwell there squat in the darkness,

dirt is their food, their drink is clay,

they are dressed in feathered garments like birds,

they never see light, and on door and bolt

the dust lies thick. When I entered that house,

I looked, and around me were piles of crowns,

I saw proud kings who had ruled the land,

who had set out roast meat before the gods

and offered cool water and cakes for the dead.

I saw high priests and acolytes squatting,

exorcists and prophets, the ecstatic and the dull,

I saw Etana, the primeval king,

Sumuqan, the wild animals' god,

and Ereshkigal, the somber queen

of the underworld. Belet-seri, her scribe,

was kneeling before her, reading from the tablet

on which each mortal's death is inscribed.

When the queen saw me, she glared and said,

'Who has brought this new resident here?' "

Gilgamesh said, "Though it *sounds* bad, this dream

may be a good omen. The gods send dreams

just to the healthy, never to the weak,

so it is a healthy man who has dreamed this.

Now I will pray to the great gods for help,

I will pray to Shamash and to your god,

to Anu, father of the gods, to Enlil

the counselor, and to Ea the wise,
I will beg them to show you mercy, then
I will have a gold statue made in your image.
Don't worry, dear friend, you will soon get better,
this votive image will restore you to health."

Enkidu said, "There is no gold statue
that can cure this illness, beloved friend.
What Enlil has decided cannot be changed.
My fate is settled. There is nothing you can do."

At the first glow of dawn, Enkidu cried out
to Shamash, he raised his head, and the tears
poured down his cheeks. "I turn to you, Lord,
since suddenly fate has turned against me.
As for that wretched trapper who found me
when I was free in the wilderness—
because he destroyed my life, destroy
his livelihood, may he go home empty,

may no animals ever enter his traps,

or if they do, may they vanish like mist,

and may he starve for bringing me here."

After he had cursed him to his heart's content,

he then cursed Shamhat, the priestess of Ishtar.

"Shamhat, I assign you an eternal fate,

I curse you with the ultimate curse, may it seize you

instantly, as it leaves my mouth.

Never may you have a home and family,

never caress a child of your own,

may your man prefer younger, prettier girls,

may he beat you as a housewife beats a rug,

may you never acquire bright alabaster

or shining silver, the delight of men,

may your roof keep leaking and no carpenter fix it,

may wild dogs camp in your bedroom, may owls

nest in your attic, may drunkards vomit

all over you, may a tavern wall

be your place of business, may you be dressed

in torn robes and filthy underwear,

may angry wives sue you, may thorns and briars

make your feet bloody, may young men jeer

and the rabble mock you as you walk the streets.

Shamhat, may all this be your reward

for seducing me in the wilderness

when I was strong and innocent and free."

Bright Shamash, the protector, heard his prayer.

Then from heaven the voice of the god

called out: "Enkidu, why are you cursing

the priestess Shamhat? Wasn't it she

who gave you fine bread fit for a god

and fine beer fit for a king, who clothed you

in a glorious robe and gave you splendid

Gilgamesh as your intimate friend?

He will lay you down on a bed of honor,

he will put you on a royal bier, on his left

he will place your statue in the seat of repose,

the princes of the earth will kiss its feet,

the people of Uruk will mourn you, and when

you are gone, he will roam the wilderness

with matted hair, in a lion skin."

When Enkidu heard this, his raging heart

grew calm. He thought of Shamhat and said,

"Shamhat, I assign you a different fate,

my mouth that cursed you will bless you now.

May you be adored by nobles and princes,

two miles away from you may your lover

tremble with excitement, one mile away

may he bite his lip in anticipation,

may the warrior long to be naked beside you,

may Ishtar give you generous lovers

whose treasure chests brim with jewels and gold,

may the mother of seven be abandoned for your sake."

Then Enkidu said to Gilgamesh,
"You who have walked beside me, steadfast
through so many dangers, remember me,
never forget what I have endured."

The day that Enkidu had his dreams,
his strength began failing. For twelve long days
he was deathly sick, he lay in his bed
in agony, unable to rest,
and every day he grew worse. At last
he sat up and called out to Gilgamesh:
"Have you abandoned me now, dear friend?
You told me that you would come to help me
when I was afraid. But I cannot see you,
you have not come to fight off this danger.
Yet weren't we to remain forever
inseparable, you and I?"

When he heard the death rattle, Gilgamesh moaned
like a dove. His face grew dark. "Beloved,
wait, don't leave me. Dearest of men,
don't die, don't let them take you from me."

BOOK VIII

All through the long night, Gilgamesh wept
for his dead friend. At the first glow of dawn,
he cried out, "Enkidu, dearest brother,
you came to Uruk from the wilderness,
your mother was a gazelle, your father
a wild ass, you were raised on the milk
of antelope and deer, and the wandering herds
taught you where the best pastures were.
May the paths that led you to the Cedar Forest
mourn you constantly, day and night,
may the elders of great-walled Uruk mourn you,
who gave us their blessing when we departed,
may the hills mourn you and the mountains we climbed,
may the pastures mourn you as their own son,
may the forest we slashed in our fury mourn you,

may the bear mourn you, the hyena, the panther,

the leopard, deer, jackal, lion, wild bull, gazelle,

may the rivers Ulaya and Euphrates mourn you,

whose sacred waters we offered to the gods,

may the young men of great-walled Uruk mourn you,

who cheered when we slaughtered the Bull of Heaven,

may the farmer mourn you, who praised you to the skies

in his harvest song, may the shepherd mourn you,

who brought you milk, may the brewer mourn you,

who made you fine beer, may Ishtar's priestess

mourn you, who massaged you with sweet-smelling oil,

may the wedding guests mourn you like their own brother,

may the temple priests mourn you, loosening their hair.

"Hear me, elders, hear me, young men,

my beloved friend is dead, he is dead,

my beloved brother is dead, I will mourn

as long as I breathe, I will sob for him

like a woman who has lost her only child.

O Enkidu, you were the axe at my side

in which my arm trusted, the knife in my sheath,

the shield I carried, my glorious robe,

the wide belt around my loins, and now

a harsh fate has torn you from me, forever.

Beloved friend, swift stallion, wild deer,

leopard ranging in the wilderness—

Enkidu, my friend, swift stallion, wild deer,

leopard ranging in the wilderness—

together we crossed the mountains, together

we slaughtered the Bull of Heaven, we killed

Humbaba, who guarded the Cedar Forest—

O Enkidu, what is this sleep that has seized you,

that has darkened your face and stopped your breath?"

But Enkidu did not answer. Gilgamesh

touched his heart, but it did not beat.

Then he veiled Enkidu's face like a bride's.

Like an eagle Gilgamesh circled around him,

he paced in front of him, back and forth,

like a lioness whose cubs are trapped in a pit,

he tore out clumps of his hair, tore off

his magnificent robes as though they were cursed.

At the first glow of dawn, Gilgamesh sent out

a proclamation: "Blacksmiths, goldsmiths,

workers in silver, metal, and gems—

create a statue of Enkidu, my friend,

make it more splendid than any statue

that has ever been made. Cover his beard

with lapis lazuli, his chest with gold.

Let obsidian and all other beautiful stones—

a thousand jewels of every color—

be piled along with the silver and gold

and sent on a barge, down the Euphrates

to great-walled Uruk, for Enkidu's statue.

I will lay him down on a bed of honor,

I will put him on a royal bier, on my left

I will place his statue in the seat of repose,

the princes of the earth will kiss its feet,

the people of Uruk will mourn him, and when

he is gone, I will roam the wilderness

with matted hair, in a lion skin."

After he sent out the proclamation,

he went to the treasury, unlocked the door

and surveyed his riches, then he brought out

priceless, jewel-studded weapons and tools,

with inlaid handles of ivory and gold,

and he heaped them up for Enkidu, his friend,

as an offering to the gods of the underworld.

He gathered fattened oxen and sheep,

he butchered them, and he piled them high

for Enkidu, his beloved friend.

He closed his eyes, in his mind he formed

an image of the infernal river,

then he opened the palace gate, brought out

an offering table of precious yew wood,

filled a carnelian bowl with honey,

filled a lapis lazuli bowl

with butter, and when the offerings were ready

he spread out each one in front of Shamash.

To the great queen Ishtar his offering was

a polished javelin of pure cedar.

"Let Ishtar accept this, let her welcome my friend

and walk at his side in the underworld,

so that Enkidu may not be sick at heart."

To Sîn, the god of the moon, he offered

a knife with a curved obsidian blade.

"Let Sîn accept this, let him welcome my friend

and walk at his side in the underworld,

so that Enkidu may not be sick at heart."

To Ereshkigal, the dark queen of the dead,

he offered a lapis lazuli flask.

"Let the queen accept this, let her welcome my friend

and walk at his side in the underworld,

so that Enkidu may not be sick at heart."

To Tammuz, the shepherd beloved by Ishtar,

his offering was a carnelian flute;

to Namtar, vizier of the dark gods,

a lapis lazuli chair and scepter;

to Hushbishag, handmaid of the dark gods,

a golden necklace; to Qassa-tabat,

the infernal sweeper, a silver bracelet;

to the housekeeper, Ninshuluhha, a mirror

of alabaster, on the back of which

was a picture of the Cedar Forest, inlaid

with rubies and lapis lazuli;

to the butcher, Bibbu, a double-edged knife

with a haft of lapis lazuli bearing

a picture of the holy Euphrates.

When all the offerings were set out, he prayed,
"Let the gods accept these, let them welcome my friend
and walk at his side in the underworld,
so that Enkidu may not be sick at heart."

After the funeral, Gilgamesh went out
from Uruk, into the wilderness
with matted hair, in a lion skin.

BOOK IX

Gilgamesh wept over Enkidu his friend,

bitterly he wept through the wilderness.

"Must I die too? Must I be as lifeless

as Enkidu? How can I bear this sorrow

that gnaws at my belly, this fear of death

that restlessly drives me onward? If only

I could find the one man whom the gods made immortal,

I would ask him how to overcome death."

So Gilgamesh roamed, his heart full of anguish,

wandering, always eastward, in search

of Utnapishtim, whom the gods made immortal.

Finally he arrived at the two high mountains

called the Twin Peaks. Their summits touch

the vault of heaven, their bases reach down

to the underworld, they keep watch over

the sun's departure and its return.

Two scorpion people were posted at the entrance,

guarding the tunnel into which the sun

plunges when it sets and moves through the earth

to emerge above the horizon at dawn.

The sight of these two inspired such terror

that it could kill an ordinary man.

Their auras shimmered over the mountains.

When Gilgamesh saw them, he was pierced with dread,

but he steadied himself and headed toward them.

The scorpion man called out to his wife,

"This one who approaches—he must be a god."

The scorpion woman called back to him,

"He is two-thirds divine and one-third human."

The scorpion man said, "What is your name?
How have you dared to come here? Why
have you traveled so far, over seas and mountains
difficult to cross, through wastelands and deserts
no mortal has ever entered? Tell me
the goal of your journey. I want to know."

"Gilgamesh is my name," he answered,
"I am the king of great-walled Uruk
and have come here to find my ancestor
Utnapishtim, who joined the assembly
of the gods, and was granted eternal life.
He is my last hope. I want to ask him
how he managed to overcome death."

The scorpion man said, "No one is able
to cross the Twin Peaks, nor has anyone ever
entered the tunnel into which the sun
plunges when it sets and moves through the earth.

Inside the tunnel there is total darkness:
deep is the darkness, with no light at all."

The scorpion woman said, "This brave man,
driven by despair, his body frost-chilled,
exhausted, and burnt by the desert sun—
show him the way to Utnapishtim."

The scorpion man said, "Ever downward
through the deep darkness the tunnel leads.
All will be pitch black before and behind you,
all will be pitch black to either side.
You must run through the tunnel faster than the wind.
You have just twelve hours. If you don't emerge
from the tunnel before the sun sets and enters,
you will find no refuge from its deadly fire.
Penetrate into the mountains' depths,
may the Twin Peaks lead you safely to your goal,
may they safely take you to the edge of the world.

The gate to the tunnel lies here before you.

Go now in peace, and return in peace."

As the sun was rising, Gilgamesh entered.

He began to run. For one hour he ran,

deep was the darkness, with no light at all

before and behind him and to either side.

For a second and a third hour Gilgamesh ran,

deep was the darkness, with no light at all

before and behind him and to either side.

For a fourth and a fifth hour Gilgamesh ran,

deep was the darkness, with no light at all

before and behind him and to either side.

For a sixth and a seventh hour Gilgamesh ran,

deep was the darkness, with no light at all

before and behind him and to either side.

At the eighth hour Gilgamesh cried out with fear,

deep was the darkness, with no light at all

before and behind him and to either side.

At the ninth hour he felt a breeze on his face,

deep was the darkness, with no light at all

before and behind him and to either side.

For a tenth and eleventh hour Gilgamesh ran,

deep was the darkness, with no light at all

before and behind him and to either side.

At the twelfth hour he emerged from the tunnel

into the light. The sun was hurtling

toward the entrance. He had barely escaped.

Before him the garden of the gods appeared,

with gem-trees of all colors, dazzling to see.

There were trees that grew rubies, trees with lapis

lazuli flowers, trees that dangled

gigantic coral clusters like dates.

Everywhere, sparkling on all the branches,

were enormous jewels: emeralds, sapphires,

hematite, diamonds, carnelians, pearls.

Gilgamesh looked up and marveled at it all.

BOOK X

At the edge of the ocean, the tavern keeper
Shiduri was sitting. Her face was veiled,
her golden pot-stand and brewing vat
stood at her side. As Gilgamesh came
toward her, worn out, his heart full of anguish,
she thought, "This desperate man must be
a murderer. Why else is he heading
straight toward me?" She rushed into her tavern,
locked the door, then climbed to the roof.
Gilgamesh heard the noise, he looked up
and saw her standing there, staring at him.
"Why did you lock yourself in?" he shouted.
"I want to enter now. If you don't let me,
I will smash your locks and break down your door."

Shiduri answered, "You seemed so wild
that I locked my door and climbed to the roof.
Tell me your name now. Where you are going?"

"Gilgamesh is my name," he said.
"I am the king of great-walled Uruk.
I am the man who killed Humbaba
in the Cedar Forest, I am the man
who triumphed over the Bull of Heaven."

Shiduri said, "Why are your cheeks so hollow
and your features so ravaged? Why is your face
frost-chilled, and burnt by the desert sun?
Why is there so much grief in your heart?
Why are you worn out and ready to collapse,
like someone who has been on a long, hard journey?"

Gilgamesh said, "Shouldn't my cheeks
be hollow, shouldn't my face be ravaged,

frost-chilled, and burnt by the desert sun?

Shouldn't my heart be filled with grief?

Shouldn't I be worn out and ready to collapse?

My friend, my brother, whom I loved so dearly,

who accompanied me through every danger—

Enkidu, my brother, whom I loved so dearly,

who accompanied me through every danger—

the fate of mankind has overwhelmed him.

For six days I would not let him be buried,

thinking, 'If my grief is violent enough,

perhaps he will come back to life again.'

For six days and seven nights I mourned him,

until a maggot fell out of his nose.

Then I was frightened, I was terrified by death,

and I set out to roam the wilderness.

I cannot bear what happened to my friend—

I cannot bear what happened to Enkidu—

so I roam the wilderness in my grief.

How can my mind have any rest?

My beloved friend has turned into clay—
my beloved Enkidu has turned into clay.
And won't I too lie down in the dirt
like him, and never arise again?"

Shiduri said, "Gilgamesh, where are you roaming?
You will never find the eternal life
that you seek. When the gods created mankind,
they also created death, and they held back
eternal life for themselves alone.
Humans are born, they live, then they die,
this is the order that the gods have decreed.
But until the end comes, enjoy your life,
spend it in happiness, not despair.
Savor your food, make each of your days
a delight, bathe and anoint yourself,
wear bright clothes that are sparkling clean,
let music and dancing fill your house,

love the child who holds you by the hand,

and give your wife pleasure in your embrace.

That is the best way for a man to live."

Gilgamesh cried out, "What are you saying,

tavern keeper? My heart is sick

for my friend who died. What can your words mean

when my heart is sick for Enkidu who died?

Show me the road to Utnapishtim.

I will cross the vast ocean if I can. If not,

I will roam the wilderness in my grief."

Shiduri said, "Never has there been a path

across the vast ocean, nor has there ever

been any human who was able to cross it.

Only brave Shamash as he climbs the sky

can cross the vast ocean—who else can do it?

The crossing is harsh, the danger is great,

and midway lie the Waters of Death,

whose touch kills instantly. Even if you manage

to sail that distance, what will you do

when you reach the Waters of Death? The one

man who can help you is Urshanabi,

Utnapishtim's boatman. He is trimming

pine branches down in the forest, and he has

the Stone Men with him. Go to him. Ask.

If he says yes, you can cross the vast ocean.

If he says no, you will have to turn back."

At these words, Gilgamesh gripped his axe,

drew his knife, and crept down toward them.

When he was close, he fell upon them

like an arrow. His battle-cry rang through the forest.

Urshanabi saw the bright knife,

saw the axe flash, and he stood there, dazed.

Fear gripped the Stone Men who crewed the boat.

Gilgamesh smashed them to pieces, then threw them

into the sea. They sank in the water.

Gilgamesh came back and stood before him.

Urshanabi stared, then he said,

"Who *are* you? Tell me. What is your name?

I am Urshanabi, the servant

of Utnapishtim, the Distant One."

"Gilgamesh is my name," he answered,

"I am the king of great-walled Uruk.

I have traveled here across the high mountains,

I have traveled here on the hidden road

through the underworld, where the sun comes forth.

Show me the way to Utnapishtim."

Urshanabi said, "Your own hands

have prevented the crossing, since in your fury

you have smashed the Stone Men, who crewed my boat

and could not be injured by the Waters of Death.

But don't despair. There is one more way

we can cross the vast ocean. Take your axe,

cut down three hundred punting poles, each

a hundred feet long, strip them, make grips,

and bring them to me. I will wait for you here."

Gilgamesh went deep into the forest,

he cut down three hundred punting poles, each

a hundred feet long, he stripped them, made grips,

and brought them to Urshanabi the boatman.

They boarded the boat and sailed away.

They sailed, without stopping, for three days and nights,

a six weeks' journey for ordinary men,

until they reached the Waters of Death.

Urshanabi said, "Now be careful,

take up the first pole, push us forward,

and do not touch the Waters of Death.

When you come to the end of the first pole, drop it,

take up a second and a third one, until

you come to the end of the three-hundredth pole

and the Waters of Death are well behind us."

When all three hundred poles had been used,

Gilgamesh took Urshanabi's robe.

He held it as a sail, with both arms extended,

and the little boat moved on toward the shore.

Alone on the shore stood Utnapishtim,

wondering as he watched them approach.

"Where are the Stone Men who crew the boat?

Why is there a stranger on board?

I have never seen him. Who can he be?"

Gilgamesh landed. When he saw the old man,

he said to him, "Tell me, where can I find

Utnapishtim, who joined the assembly
of the gods, and was granted eternal life?"

Utnapishtim said, "Why are your cheeks
so hollow? Why is your face so ravaged,
frost-chilled, and burnt by the desert sun?
Why is there so much grief in your heart?
Why are you worn out and ready to collapse,
like someone who has been on a long, hard journey?"

Gilgamesh said, "Shouldn't my cheeks
be hollow, shouldn't my face be ravaged,
frost-chilled, and burnt by the desert sun?
Shouldn't my heart be filled with grief?
Shouldn't I be worn out and ready to collapse?
My friend, my brother, whom I loved so dearly,
who accompanied me through every danger—
Enkidu, my brother, whom I loved so dearly,
who accompanied me through every danger—

the fate of mankind has overwhelmed him.

For six days I would not let him be buried,

thinking, 'If my grief is violent enough,

perhaps he will come back to life again.'

For six days and seven nights I mourned him,

until a maggot fell out of his nose.

Then I was frightened, I was terrified by death,

and I set out to roam the wilderness.

I cannot bear what happened to my friend—

I cannot bear what happened to Enkidu—

so I roam the wilderness in my grief.

How can my mind have any rest?

My beloved friend has turned into clay—

my beloved Enkidu has turned into clay.

And won't I too lie down in the dirt

like him, and never arise again?

That is why I must find Utnapishtim,

whom men call 'The Distant One.' I must ask him

how he managed to overcome death.

I have wandered the world, climbed the most treacherous

mountains, crossed deserts, sailed the vast ocean,

and sweet sleep has rarely softened my face.

I have worn myself out through ceaseless striving,

I have filled my muscles with pain and anguish.

I have killed bear, lion, hyena, leopard,

tiger, deer, antelope, ibex, I have eaten

their meat and have wrapped their rough skins around me.

And what in the end have I achieved?

When I reached Shiduri the tavern keeper,

I was filthy, exhausted, heartsick. Now let

the gate of sorrow be closed behind me,

and let it be sealed shut with tar and pitch."

Utnapishtim said, "Gilgamesh, why

prolong your grief? Have you ever paused

to compare your own blessed lot with a fool's?

You were made from the flesh of both gods and humans,

the gods have lavished you with their gifts

as though they were your fathers and mothers,

from your birth they assigned you a throne and told you,

'Rule over men!' To the fool they gave

beer dregs instead of butter, stale crusts

instead of bread that is fit for gods,

rags instead of magnificent garments,

instead of a wide fringed belt an old rope,

and a frantic, senseless, dissatisfied mind.

Can't you see how fortunate you are?

You have worn yourself out through ceaseless striving,

you have filled your muscles with pain and anguish.

And what have you achieved but to bring yourself

one day nearer to the end of your days?

At night the moon travels across the sky,

the gods of heaven stay awake and watch us,

unsleeping, undying. This is the way

the world is established, from ancient times.

✿

"Yes: the gods took Enkidu's life.

But man's life *is* short, at any moment

it can be snapped, like a reed in a canebrake.

The handsome young man, the lovely young woman—

in their prime, death comes and drags them away.

Though no one has seen death's face or heard

death's voice, suddenly, savagely, death

destroys us, all of us, old or young.

And yet we build houses, make contracts, brothers

divide their inheritance, conflicts occur—

as though this human life lasted forever.

The river rises, flows over its banks

and carries us all away, like mayflies

floating downstream: they stare at the sun,

then all at once there is nothing.

"The sleeper and the dead, how alike they are!

Yet the sleeper wakes up and opens his eyes,

while no one returns from death. And who

can know when the last of his days will come?

When the gods assemble, they decide your fate,

they establish both life and death for you,

but the time of death they do not reveal."

BOOK XI

Gilgamesh said to Utnapishtim,

"I imagined that you would look like a god.

But you look like me, you are not any different.

I intended to fight you, yet now that I stand

before you, now that I see who you are,

I can't fight, something is holding me back.

Tell me, how is it that you, a mortal,

overcame death and joined the assembly

of the gods and were granted eternal life?"

Utnapishtim said, "I will tell you

a mystery, a secret of the gods.

You know Shuruppak, that ancient city

on the Euphrates. I lived there once.

I was its king once, a long time ago,

when the great gods decided to send the Flood.

Five gods decided, and they took an oath

to keep the plan secret: Anu their father,

the counselor Enlil, Ninurta the gods'

chamberlain, and Ennugi the sheriff.

Ea also, the cleverest of the gods,

had taken the oath, but I heard him whisper

the secret to the reed fence around my house.

'Reed fence, reed fence, listen to my words.

King of Shuruppak, quickly, quickly

tear down your house and build a great ship,

leave your possessions, save your life.

The ship must be square, so that its length

equals its width. Build a roof over it,

just as the Great Deep is covered by the earth.

Then gather and take aboard the ship

examples of every living creature.'

"I understood Ea's words, and I said,

'My lord, I will obey your command,

exactly as you have spoken it.

But what shall I say when the people ask me

why I am building such a large ship?'

"Ea said, 'Tell them that Enlil hates you,

that you can no longer live in their city

or walk on the earth, which belongs to Enlil,

that it is your fate to go down into

the Great Deep and live with Ea your lord,

and that Ea will rain abundance upon them.

They will all have all that they want, and more.'

"I laid out the structure, I drafted plans.

At the first glow of dawn, everyone gathered—

carpenters brought their saws and axes,

reed workers brought their flattening-stones,

rope makers brought their ropes, and children

carried the tar. The poor helped also,

however they could—some carried timber,

some hammered nails, some cut wood.

By the end of the fifth day the hull had been built:

the decks were an acre large, the sides

two hundred feet high. I built six decks,

so that the ship's height was divided in seven.

I divided each deck into nine compartments,

drove water plugs into all the holes,

brought aboard spars and other equipment,

had three thousand gallons of tar poured into

the furnace, and three thousand gallons of pitch

poured out. The bucket carriers brought

three thousand gallons of oil—a thousand

were used for the caulking, two thousand were left,

which the boatman stored. Each day I slaughtered

bulls for my workmen, I slaughtered sheep,

I gave them barrels of beer and ale

and wine, and they drank it like river water.

When all our work on the ship was finished,
we feasted as though it were New Year's Day.
At sunrise I handed out oil for the ritual,
by sunset the ship was ready. The launching
was difficult. We rolled her on logs
down to the river and eased her in
until two-thirds was under the water.
I loaded onto her everything precious
that I owned: all my silver and gold,
all my family, all my kinfolk,
all kinds of animals, wild and tame,
craftsmen and artisans of every kind.

"Then Shamash announced that the time had come.
'Enter the ship now. Seal the hatch.'
I gazed at the sky—it was terrifying.
I entered the ship. To Puzur-amurri
the shipwright, the man who sealed the hatch,
I gave my palace, with all its contents.

❀

"At the first glow of dawn, an immense black cloud

rose on the horizon and crossed the sky.

Inside it the storm god Adad was thundering,

while Shullat and Hanish, twin gods of destruction,

went first, tearing through mountains and valleys.

Nergal, the god of pestilence, ripped out

the dams of the Great Deep, Ninurta opened

the floodgates of heaven, the infernal gods

blazed and set the whole land on fire.

A deadly silence spread through the sky

and what had been bright now turned to darkness.

The land was shattered like a clay pot.

All day, ceaselessly, the storm winds blew,

the rain fell, then the Flood burst forth,

overwhelming the people like war.

No one could see through the rain, it fell

harder and harder, so thick that you couldn't

see your own hand before your eyes.

Even the gods were afraid. The water

rose higher and higher until the gods fled

to Anu's palace in the highest heaven.

But Anu had shut the gates. The gods

cowered by the palace wall, like dogs.

"Sweet-voiced Aruru, mother of men,

screamed out, like a woman in childbirth:

'If only that day had never been,

when I spoke up for evil in the council of the gods!

How could I have agreed to destroy

my children by sending the Great Flood upon them?

I have given birth to the human race, only

to see them fill the ocean like fish.'

The other gods were lamenting with her.

They sat and listened to her and wept.

Their lips were parched, crusted with scabs.

"For six days and seven nights, the storm

demolished the earth. On the seventh day,

the downpour stopped. The ocean grew calm.

No land could be seen, just water on all sides,

as flat as a roof. There was no life at all.

The human race had turned into clay.

I opened a hatch and the blessed sunlight

streamed upon me, I fell to my knees

and wept. When I got up and looked around,

a coastline appeared, a half mile away.

On Mount Nimush the ship ran aground,

the mountain held it and would not release it.

For six days and seven nights, the mountain

would not release it. On the seventh day,

I brought out a dove and set it free.

The dove flew off, then flew back to the ship,

because there was no place to land. I waited,

then I brought out a swallow and set it free.

The swallow flew off, then flew back to the ship,

because there was no place to land. I waited,

then I brought out a raven and set it free.

The raven flew off, and because the water

had receded, it found a branch, it sat there,

it ate, it flew off and didn't return.

"When the waters had dried up and land appeared,

I set free the animals I had taken,

I slaughtered a sheep on the mountaintop

and offered it to the gods, I arranged

two rows of seven ritual vases,

I burned reeds, cedar, and myrtle branches.

The gods smelled the fragrance, they smelled the sweet fragrance

and clustered around the offering like flies.

"When Aruru came, she held up in the air

her necklace of lapis lazuli,

Anu's gift when their love was new.

'I swear by this precious ornament

that never will I forget these days.

Let all the gods come to the sacrifice,

except for Enlil, because he recklessly

sent the Great Flood and destroyed my children.'

"Then Enlil arrived. When he saw the ship,

he was angry, he raged at the other gods.

'Who helped these humans escape? Wasn't

the Flood supposed to destroy them all?'

"Ninurta answered, 'Who else but Ea,

the cleverest of us, could devise such a thing?'

"Ea said to the counselor Enlil,

'You, the wisest and bravest of the gods,

how did it happen that you so recklessly

sent the Great Flood to destroy mankind?

It is right to punish the sinner for his sins,

to punish the criminal for his crime,

but be merciful, do not allow all men

to die because of the sins of some.

Instead of a flood, you should have sent

lions to decimate the human race,

or wolves, or a famine, or a deadly plague.

As for my taking the solemn oath,

I didn't reveal the secret of the gods,

I only whispered it to a fence

and Utnapishtim happened to hear.

Now *you* must decide what his fate will be.'

"Then Enlil boarded, he took my hand,

he led me out, then he led out my wife.

He had us kneel down in front of him,

he touched our foreheads and, standing between us,

he blessed us. 'Hear me, you gods: Until now,

Utnapishtim was a mortal man.

But from now on, he and his wife shall be

gods like us, they shall live forever,

at the source of the rivers, far away.'

Then they brought us to this distant place

at the source of the rivers. Here we live.

"Now then, Gilgamesh, who will assemble

the gods for *your* sake? Who will convince them

to grant you the eternal life that you seek?

How would they know that you deserve it?

First pass this test: Just stay awake

for seven days. Prevail against sleep,

and perhaps you will prevail against death."

So Gilgamesh sat down against a wall

to begin the test. The moment he sat down,

sleep swirled over him, like a fog.

Utnapishtim said to his wife,

"Look at this fellow! He wanted to live

forever, but the very moment he sat down,

sleep swirled over him, like a fog."

His wife said, "Touch him on the shoulder, wake him,

let him depart and go back safely

to his own land, by the gate he came through."

Utnapishtim said, "All men are liars.

When he wakes up, watch how he tries to deceive us.

So bake a loaf for each day he sleeps,

put them in a row beside him, and make

a mark on the wall for every loaf."

She baked the loaves and put them beside him,

she made a mark for each day he slept.

The first loaf was rock-hard, the second loaf

was dried out like leather, the third had shrunk,

the fourth had a whitish covering, the fifth

was spotted with mold, the sixth was stale,

the seventh loaf was still on the coals

when he reached out and touched him. Gilgamesh

woke with a start and said, "I was almost

falling asleep when I felt your touch."

Utnapishtim said, "Look down, friend,

count these loaves that my wife baked and put here

while you sat sleeping. This first one, rock-hard,

was baked seven days ago, this leathery one

was baked six days ago, and so on for all

the rest of the days you sat here sleeping.

Look. They are marked on the wall behind you."

Gilgamesh cried out, "What shall I do,

where shall I go now? Death has caught me,

it lurks in my bedroom, and everywhere I look,

everywhere I turn, there is only death."

Utnapishtim said to the boatman,

"This is the last time, Urshanabi,

that you are allowed to cross the vast ocean

and reach these shores. As for this man,

he is filthy and tired, his hair is matted,

animal skins have obscured his beauty.

Bring him to the tub and wash out his hair,

take off his animal skin and let

the waves of the ocean carry it away,

moisten his body with sweet-smelling oil,

bind his hair in a bright new headband,

dress him in fine robes fit for a king.

Until he comes to the end of his journey

let his robes be spotless, as though they were new."

He brought him to the tub, he washed out his hair,

he took off his animal skin and let

the waves of the ocean carry it away,

he moistened his body with sweet-smelling oil,

he bound his hair in a bright new headband,

he dressed him in fine robes fit for a king.

Then Gilgamesh and Urshanabi

boarded, pushed off, and the little boat

began to move away from the shore.

But the wife of Utnapishtim said, "Wait,

this man came a very long way, he endured

many hardships to get here. Won't you

give him something for his journey home?"

When he heard this, Gilgamesh turned the boat

around, and he brought it back to the shore.

Utnapishtim said, "Gilgamesh,

you came a very long way, you endured

many hardships to get here. Now

I will give you something for your journey home,

a mystery, a secret of the gods.

There is a small spiny bush that grows

in the waters of the Great Deep, it has sharp spikes

that will prick your fingers like a rose's thorns.

If you find this plant and bring it to the surface,

you will have found the secret of youth."

Gilgamesh dug a pit on the shore

that led down into the Great Deep. He tied

two heavy stones to his feet, they pulled him

downward into the water's depths.

He found the plant, he grasped it, it tore

his fingers, they bled, he cut off the stones,

his body shot up to the surface, and the waves

cast him back, gasping, onto the shore.

Gilgamesh said to Urshanabi,

"Come here, look at this marvelous plant,

the antidote to the fear of death.

With it we return to the youth we once had.

I will take it to Uruk, I will test its power

by seeing what happens when an old man eats it.

If that succeeds, I will eat some myself

and become a carefree young man again."

At four hundred miles they stopped to eat,

at a thousand miles they pitched their camp.

Gilgamesh saw a pond of cool water.

He left the plant on the ground and bathed.

A snake smelled its fragrance, stealthily

it crawled up and carried the plant away.

As it disappeared, it cast off its skin.

When Gilgamesh saw what the snake had done,

he sat down and wept. He said to the boatman,

"What shall I do now? All my hardships

have been for nothing. O Urshanabi,

was it for this that my hands have labored,

was it for this that I gave my heart's blood?

I have gained no benefit for myself

but have lost the marvelous plant to a reptile.

I plucked it from the depths, and how could I ever

manage to find that place again?

And our little boat—we left it on the shore."

At four hundred miles they stopped to eat,

at a thousand miles they pitched their camp.

When at last they arrived, Gilgamesh

said to Urshanabi, "This is

the wall of Uruk, which no city on earth can equal.

See how its ramparts gleam like copper in the sun.

Climb the stone staircase, more ancient than the mind can imagine,

approach the Eanna Temple, sacred to Ishtar,

a temple that no king has equaled in size or beauty,

walk on the wall of Uruk, follow its course

around the city, inspect its mighty foundations,

examine its brickwork, how masterfully it is built,

observe the land it encloses: the palm trees, the gardens,

the orchards, the glorious palaces and temples, the shops

and marketplaces, the houses, the public squares."

NOTES

INTRODUCTION

p. 1, *Enkidu:* The accent (as with Gilgamesh) is on the first syllable.

p. 3, *he wrote at the end of 1916:* "*Gilgamesh* is stupendous! I know it from the edition of the original text and consider it to be among the greatest things that can happen to a person. From time to time I tell it to people, I tell the whole story, and every time I have the most astonished listeners. The synthesis of Burckhardt is not altogether fortunate, it doesn't achieve the greatness and significance of the original. I feel that I tell it better. And it suits me" (to Katharina Kippenberg, December 11, 1916, *Briefwechsel: Rainer Maria Rilke und Katharina Kippenberg,* Insel Verlag, 1954, p. 191). "Have you seen the volume published by Insel Books, that somewhat like a *résumé* contains an ancient Assyrian poem: the *Gilgamesh.* I have immersed myself in the literal scholarly translation (of Ungnad), and in these truly gigantic fragments I have experienced measures and forms that belong with the supreme works that the conjuring Word has ever produced. I would really prefer to tell it to you—the little Insel book, tastefully produced though it is, doesn't convey the real power of the five-thousand-year-old poem. In the (I must admit, excellently translated) fragments there is a truly colossal happening and being and fearing, and even the wide gaps in the text function somehow constructively, in that they keep the gloriously massive surfaces apart. Here is the epic of the fear of death, arisen in the immemorial among people who were the first for whom the separation between life and death became definitive and fateful. I am sure that your husband too will have the liveliest joy in reading through these pages. I have been living for weeks almost entirely in this impression [of them]" (to Helene von Nostitz, New Year's Eve, 1916, *Briefwechsel mit Helene von Nostitz,* Insel Verlag, 1976, p. 99).

p. 3, *Austen Henry Layard:* "The French were first in the field in 1842 at Nineveh and, from 1843, at Khorsabad, the eighth-century-BC capital of the Assyrian king Sargon II. But they were soon outshone and outmaneuvered by a young British traveler and adventurer, Austen Henry Layard. En route to Ceylon, the twenty-eight-year-old Layard became intrigued with stories of buried remains in the mounds near present-day Mosul which turned out to be ancient Nineveh and Nimrud, the two most fabled capitals of the Assyrians.

"Within days of starting the digging at Nimrud, Layard hit upon the first of eight palaces of the Assyrian kings dating from the ninth to seventh centuries BC, which he and his assistant eventually uncovered there and at Nineveh. In amazement they found room after room lined with carved stone bas-reliefs of demons and deities, scenes of battle, royal hunts and ceremonies; doorways flanked by enormous winged bulls and lions; and, inside some of the chambers, tens of thousands of clay tablets inscribed with the curious, and then undeciphered, cuneiform ('wedge-shaped') script—the remains, as we now know, of scholarly libraries assembled by the Assyrian kings Sennacherib and Ashurbanipal. By later standards it was treasure-hunting rather than archaeology, but after a few years of excavation in difficult political and financial circumstances,

Layard had succeeded in resurrecting for the first time one of the great early cultures of Mesopotamia. He never made it to Ceylon.

"The most spectacular finds were shipped back to the British Museum, where the Victorian fascination with the Bible assured these illustrations of Old Testament history a rapturous reception. By the early 1850s, progress in reading the Assyrian-Babylonian script had allowed names and events to be attached to the images, among them Jehu, the ninth-century-BC king of Israel (shown paying obeisance to King Shalmanesser III), and the siege of Lachish in Judah by Sennacherib. Layard's account of his discoveries, *Nineveh and Its Remains* (1849), soon had a huge success: 'the greatest achievement of our time,' according to Lord Ellesmere, president of the Royal Asiatic Society. 'No man living has done so much or told it so well.' An abridged edition (1852) prepared for the series 'Murray's Reading for the Rail' became an instant best seller: the first year's sales of eight thousand (as Layard remarked in a letter) 'will place it side by side with *Mrs. Rundell's Cookery.*'

"Work on the decipherment of the language of the Assyrian inscriptions was making good progress while Layard was in the field, partly owing to his discoveries. But the key to cracking the cuneiform script lay elsewhere—in a trilingual inscription of the Persian king Darius carved on the face of a cliff at Behistun in western Iran around 520 BC. (In all, the cuneiform script was used for over 3,500 years.) One of the three versions of the text used a much simpler cuneiform script with only around forty characters, which scholars soon realized must be alphabetic. Even before Layard's excavations, by making some inspired guesses about likely titles and names, they had deciphered this script and shown the language to be Old Persian, thus of the Indo-Iranian language family (a close relative of Indo-European). Having determined the general meaning of the three texts, scholars now confirmed that the second version, written in the much more complex cuneiform script (some three hundred characters) of the tablets from Assyria, was, as many had suspected, a Semitic language (i.e., cognate with Hebrew, Aramaic, and Arabic)—what we now know as Babylonian. Many texts could be read reasonably well by the time Layard's finds started arriving in England, but the decipherment was not officially declared to have been achieved until 1857, when four of the leading experts (including W. H. Fox-Talbot, one of the inventors of photography) submitted independent translations of a new inscription and all were shown to be in broad agreement. After two and a half millennia, the Assyrians had again found their voice" (Timothy Potts, "Buried between the Rivers," *New York Review of Books,* September 25, 2003). See also Sir E. A. Wallis Budge, *The Rise and Progress of Assyriology,* Martin Hopkinson, 1925, pp. 68 ff.

p. 4, *Akkadian:* The name "Akkadian" is derived from the city-state of Akkad (near present-day Baghdad), founded in the middle of the third millennium BCE and capital of one of the first great empires in human history. By 2000 BCE Akkadian had supplanted Sumerian as the major spoken language of Mesopotamia, and around this time it split into two dialects: Babylonian, which was spoken in southern Mesopotamia, and Assyrian, which was spoken in the north.

p. 4, *"On looking down the third column:* George Smith, *The Chaldean Account of Genesis,* Sampson Low, Marston, Searle and Rivington, 1876, p. 4. "I then proceeded," Smith's account continues, "to read through this document, and found it was in the form of a speech from the hero of the Deluge to a person whose name appeared to be Izdubar (=Gilgamesh; Smith was guessing [mistakenly, as it turned out] that the three cuneiform signs that formed the name had their most common syllabic values). I recollected a legend belonging to the same hero Izdubar K. 231, which, on comparison, proved to belong to the same series, and I then commenced a search for any missing portions of the tablets. This search was a long and heavy work, for there were thousands of fragments to go over, and, while on the one side I had gained as yet only two fragments of the Izdubar legends to judge from, on the other hand, the unsorted fragments were so small, and contained so little of the subject, that it was extremely difficult to ascertain their meaning. My search, however, proved successful. I found a fragment of another copy of the Deluge, containing again the sending forth of the birds, and gradually collected several other portions of this tablet, fitting them in one after another until I had completed the greater part of the second column. Portions of a third copy next turned up, which, when joined together, completed a considerable part of the first and sixth columns. I now had the account of the Deluge in the state in which I published it at the meeting of the Society of Biblical Archaeology, December 3rd, 1872."

p. 4, *according to a later account:* Budge, *The Rise and Progress of Assyriology,* p. 153.

p. 5, *caused a major stir:* "The London *Daily Telegraph* offered to fund an expedition to look for the missing part of the tablet. Smith duly set out, and on only his fifth day of searching through the spoil heaps of Nineveh—with luck that must have seemed divinely inspired—found a tablet fragment that filled most of the gap in the story" (Potts, "Buried between the Rivers").

p. 5, *Though to a modern reader it seems quaint:* Here are two examples from Tablet I (the first passage in each example is a literal prose version, the second is Smith's translation):

> Gilgamesh said to him, to the trapper, "Go, trapper, and take the *ḫarimtu* [sacred prostitute] Shamhat with you. When the animals come down to the waterhole, have her take off her robe and expose her vagina. When he sees her, he will approach. The animals will be estranged from him, though he grew up in their presence." The trapper went off, he took the *ḫarimtu* Shamhat with him, they set out on the journey. On the third day they reached their destination. The trapper and the *ḫarimtu* sat down to wait. A first and a second day they sat by the waterhole as the animals came to drink at the waterhole. The animals arrived, their hearts grew pleased, then Enkidu as well, who was born in the wilderness, who ate grass with the gazelles. He came to drink at the waterhole with the animals, his heart grew pleased as he drank the water with the animals. Shamhat saw him, this primordial being, this savage from the midst of the wilderness. "Look, Shamhat, there he is. Bare your breasts, expose your vagina, let him take in your voluptuousness. Do not hold back, take his breath. When he sees you, he will approach. Spread out your robe so that he can lie on you, do for him the work of a woman. Let him mount you in his lust, and the animals will be estranged from him, though he grew up in their presence" (I, 161 ff.).

Izdubar to him also said to Zaidu: / go Zaidu and with thee the female Harimtu, and Samhat take, / and when the beast . . . in front of the field

(directions to the female how to entice Heabani [=Enkidu])

Zaidu went and with him Harimtu, and Samhat he took, and /
they took the road, and went along the path. / On the third day
they reached the land where the flood happened. / Zaidu and
Harimtu in their places sat, the first day and the second day in
front of the field they sat, / the land where the beast drank of
drink, / the land where the creeping things of the water rejoiced
his heart. / And he Heabani had made for himself a mountain /
with the gazelles he eat food, / with the beasts he drank of drink, /
with the creeping things of the waters his heart rejoiced. Samhat
the enticer of men saw him

(details of the actions of the female Samhat and Heabani)

(*The Chaldean Account of Genesis,* p. 202). A few pages later, Smith com-
ments, "I have omitted some of the details in columns III. and IV.
because they were on the one side obscure, and on the other hand hardly
adapted for general reading."

The second passage comes from later in Tablet I. Smith's translation
is quite fragmentary:

"I will challenge him, mighty [. . .]. [. . .] in Uruk: 'I am the
mightiest! [. . .] I will change the order of things, [the one] born
in the wilderness is the strongest of all!"

"Let [him] see your face, [I will lead you to Gilgamesh,] I
know where he will be. Come, Enkidu, to Uruk-the-Sheepfold,
where the young men are girt with wide belts. Every day [. . .] a
festival is held, the lyre and drum are played, the *ḥarīmāti* stand
around, lovely, laughing, filled with sexual joy, so that even old men
are aroused from their beds. Enkidu, [you who don't yet] know life,

I will show you Gilgamesh, the man of joy and grief. You will look at him, you will see how handsome and virile he is, how his whole body is filled with sexual joy. He is even stronger than you—he doesn't sleep day or night. Put aside your audacity, Enkidu. Shamash loves Gilgamesh, and his mind has been enlarged by Anu, Enlil, and Ea [the three principal gods]." (I, 221 ff.)

I will meet him and see his power, / I will bring to the midst of Erech a tiger [!—S.M.], / and if he is able he will destroy it. / In the desert it is begotten, it has great strength, / . . . . . . before thee / . . . . . . everything there is I know / Heabani went to the midst of Erech Suburi / . . . . . . the chiefs . . . made submission / in that day they made a festival / . . . . . . city / . . . . . . daughter / . . . . . . made rejoicing / . . . . . . becoming great / . . . . . mingled and / . . . . . . Izdubar rejoicing the people / went before him / A prince thou becomest glory thou hast / . . . . . . fills his body / . . . . . . who day and night / . . . . . . destroy thy terror / . . . . . . the god Samas loves him and / . . . . . . and Hea have given intelligence to his ears.

(*The Chaldean Account of Genesis,* pp. 203–204.)

p. 5, *here is the consensus:* In the following account, through p. 6, I rely heavily on Andrew George's judicious and informative introduction to *The Epic of Gilgamesh* (hereafter abbreviated as *EG*).

p. 5, *five separate and independent poems in Sumerian:* Translations of all five poems are posted on the Sumerian Literature site of the Oriental Institute, University of Oxford, at http://www-etcsl.orient.ox.ac.uk.

p. 5, *as distant from Akkadian:* "aussi loin de l'akkadien que le chinois peut l'être du français" (Bottéro, p. 19).

p. 6, *the eleven clay tablets dug up at Nineveh:* "The 'series of Gilgamesh,' in fact, comprises twelve tablets, not just the eleven of the epic. Tablet XII, the last, is a line-by-line translation of the latter half of one of the Sumerian Gilgamesh poems . . . Most scholars would agree that it does not belong to the text but was attached to it because it was plainly related material" (George, *EG,* p. xxviii; for an extended discussion, see A. R. George, *The Babylonian Gilgamesh Epic,* I, pp. 47 ff., hereafter abbreviated as *BGE*).

p.6, *the first* Epic of Gilgamesh: "The Akkadian epic was given its original shape in the Old Babylonian Period by an Akkadian author who took over, in greater or lesser degree, the plots and themes of three or four of the Sumerian tales . . . Either translating freely from Sumerian or working from available paraphrases, the author combined these plots and themes into a unified epic on a grand scale. As the central idea in this epic, the author seized upon a theme which was adumbrated in three of the Sumerian tales, Gilgamesh's concern with death and his futile desire to overcome it. The author advanced this theme to a central position in the story. To this end, Enkidu's death became the pivotal event which set Gilgamesh on a feverish search for the immortal flood hero (whose story existed in Sumerian, but had nothing to do with the tales about Gilgamesh), hoping to learn how he had overcome death. The author separated the themes of Enkidu's death and Gilgamesh's grief from their original context in the Sumerian 'Gilgamesh, Enkidu, and the Nether-world' and placed them after the friends' victory over Huwawa (and possibly over the Bull of Heaven). To increase the emotional impact that

Enkidu's death had on Gilgamesh, and perhaps to make the depth of Gilgamesh's grief more plausible, the author seized upon one or two references to Enkidu in the Sumerian sources as Gilgamesh's friend, rather than servant, and treated him consistently as Gilgamesh's friend and equal. He even went so far as to compose accounts of Gilgamesh's oppression of Uruk, and Enkidu's creation and early life, in order to explain why Enkidu was created and how he became Gilgamesh's friend" (Tigay, pp. 242 ff.).

p. 6, *Sîn-lēqi-unninni:* His name means "Sîn [the moon god] is the One Who Accepts a Prayer" (or less probably, according to George, the name is Sîn-liqe-unninnī, "O Sîn, Accept my Prayer!"). "The first-millennium catalogue of cuneiform literature which says that 'the series *Gilgamesh* (is) according to Sîn-lēqi-unninni the ex[orcist-priest]' . . . was doubtless understood to mean that Sîn-lēqi-unninni was the author of the late version, since that was the only version known in that period. The very fact that the epic is attributed to him indicates that Sîn-lēqi-unninni must have made some important, perhaps definitive, contribution to its formulation. It is certainly possible that he was the editor of the late version, but that is not necessarily the case. It often happens that a work of literature is attributed to a figure who made a decisive contribution to its development, even though a later form of that work is the one actually in use . . . It is possible that Sîn-lēqi-unninni produced a Middle Babylonian form of *Gilgamesh* which had a substantial enough influence on the final form of the epic to associate his name with it permanently, but that the form found in the first-millennium copies was a later revision of Sîn-lēqi-unninni's text. Still, it is equally possible that he was the editor of the late version" (Tigay, p. 246).

p. 6, *Standard Version:* The Standard Version "is known from a total of 73 manuscripts extant: the 35 that have survived from the libraries of King Ashurbanipal at Nineveh, 8 more tablets and fragments from three other Assyrian cities (Ashur, Kalah and Huzirina), and 30 from Babylonia, especially the cities of Babylon and Uruk . . . The eleven tablets of the epic vary in length from 183 to 326 lines of poetry so that the whole composition would originally have been about 3,000 lines long [the same length as *Beowulf*—S.M.]. As the text now stands, only Tablets I, VI, X and XI are more or less complete. Leaving aside lines that are lost but can be restored from parallel passages, overall about 575 lines are still completely missing, that is, they are not represented by so much as a single word. Many more are too badly damaged to be useful, so that considerably less than the four-fifths of the epic that is extant yields a consecutive text" (George, *EG*, pp. xxvii–xxviii).

p. 7, *the priestess Shamhat's speech inviting Enkidu to Uruk:* This passage provides us with the only extended comparison of Sîn-lēqi-unninni's marvelous powers of expansion. Here is a literal prose translation of the Old Babylonian version (from the Pennsylvania tablet, OB II, ll. 45 ff.):

> Enkidu sat in front of the *ḫarīmtu*. The two of them made love. He forgot the wilderness where he was born. For seven days and seven nights Enkidu stayed erect and made love to Shamkatum. The *ḫarīmtu* opened her mouth and said to Enkidu, "When I look at you, Enkidu, you are like a god. Why should you roam the wilderness with the animals? Come, let me take you to Uruk of the Great Square, to the sacred temple, the home of Anu. Enkidu, get up, let me take you to Eanna, the home of Anu. [The next three lines are difficult. George restores and translates them as follows:]

Where [men] are engaged in labors of skill, you too [*like a*] *true man*, will [*make a place for*] yourself. You are familiar (enough) with the territory where the shepherd *dwells.*"

And here is Sîn-lēqi-unninni's version (again in a literal prose translation):

He embraced her with passion; for six days and seven nights Enkidu stayed erect, he made love to her until he had had enough of her delights. Then he stood up and walked toward his animals. But the gazelles saw Enkidu and scattered, the wild animals took flight. Enkidu had spent himself, his body was limp, his knees stood still while his animals went away. Enkidu was diminished, he could no longer run as he had before. He turned back to Shamhat, and as he walked he knew that his mind had grown larger. He sat down at Shamhat's feet, he looked at her intently, and he listened carefully to what she said, as she said to him, to Enkidu, "You are handsome, Enkidu, you are like a god. Why should you roam the wilderness with the animals? Let me take you to Uruk-the-Sheepfold, to the sacred temple, the dwelling of Anu and Ishtar, where Gilgamesh is mighty and oppresses the people like a wild bull."

She spoke to him, and Enkidu agreed with what she said. He became aware of a longing for a friend. Enkidu said to her, to the *ḥarīmtu*, "Come, Shamhat, lead me to the sacred temple, the holy dwelling of Anu and Ishtar, where Gilgamesh is mighty and oppresses the people like a wild bull. I will challenge him, mighty [. . .]. [. . .] in Uruk: 'I am the mightiest! [. . .] I will change the order of things, [the one] born in the wilderness is the strongest of all!"

"Let [him] see your face, [I will lead you to Gilgamesh,] I know where he will be. Come, Enkidu, to Uruk-the-Sheepfold, where the young men are girt with wide belts. Every day [. . .] a festival is held, the lyre and drum are played, the *ḫarimāti* stand around, lovely, laughing, filled with sexual joy, so that even old men are aroused from their beds. Enkidu, [you who don't yet] know life, I will show you Gilgamesh, the man of joy and grief. You will look at him, you will see how handsome and virile he is, how his whole body is filled with sexual joy. He is even stronger than you—he doesn't sleep day or night. Put aside your audacity, Enkidu. Shamash loves Gilgamesh, and his mind has been enlarged by Anu, Enlil, and Ea." (I, 193 ff.)

p. 8, *Uruk's then famous six-mile-long wall:* "Excavations have shown that by the Early Dynastic Period, that is, just about the time of the historical Gilgamesh, the walls of Uruk had a perimeter of six miles. The great area of the city at that time, the end of what archeologists call the Uruk Period (ca. 3800 B.C. to about the time of the earliest pictographs, ca. 3000 B.C.), shows that the city was probably without equal in size and wealth. Within the walls, excavators have found, about a third of the area was occupied by public buildings and the dwellings of the wealthy, about a third by houses of the poor, and a third by gardens, open spaces, and cemeteries" (Maier in Gardner and Maier, p. 61).

p. 8, *observe the land it encloses:* "The uniqueness of what happened in early Sumer and its significance for world history can hardly be exaggerated. The main source of this revolution seems to have been the city of Uruk (biblical Erech, modern Warka) in southern Sumer, which by circa 3400 BC had become the largest permanent urban settlement ever created. At its core lay two monumental temple complexes dedicated to the sky-god

Anu and the goddess of love and war, Inanna. In and around these tem-
ples were found what are still the earliest writings from anywhere in the
world, the pictographic system of recording on clay tablets that evolved
into cuneiform, along with sophisticated architectural, technological,
and artistic traditions illustrated by the Warka Vase and Head. Life in
and around the temples was supported by well-coordinated religious,
social, and presumably political administrations" (Potts, "Buried
between the Rivers").

"At the high point of its development in the fourth and third mil-
lennia, the city enclosed a territory of approximately 5.5 km² [=2.1
square miles]. The gigantic dimensions may be illustrated by a compar-
ison: Athens under Themistocles measured about 2.5 km² [=.98 square
miles], Jerusalem in the year 43 C.E. about 1 km² [=.39 square miles]; not
until Rome under Hadrian was there a city larger than Uruk" (trans-
lated from Robert Rollinger, in Schrott, p. 283).

p. 9, *the copper box / that is marked with his name:* "Under the foundations of the
main buildings, temples or palaces, people used to bury caskets containing
'foundation documents' inscribed in the name of the king who was the
builder. Gilgamesh is thus supposed to have written down his lofty deeds,
in a sort of autobiographical account, on a precious 'tablet of lapis lazuli,'
whose text might be more or less identical to that of the 'stone tablets'
referred to above. By presenting things in this way, the author of *Gílgameš*
gave (fictitiously!) as a guarantee of his book a text that originated from
the very hand of his hero" (translated from Bottéro, p. 65).

p. 10, *like the Israelite slaves in Exodus:* Exodus 2:23 ff.

p. 11, *a help meet for him:* Genesis 2:18.

p. 11, *he drives away marauding predators:* "You were raised in the mountains, with your own hands / you have killed marauding lions and wolves" (Book III, p. 94).

p. 12, *"Go to the temple of Ishtar* through *will leave him forever:* For a literal translation of this passage, see note, p. 206.

p. 13, *In opening to the anonymous man:* Much later, in the fifth century BCE, Herodotus described (or invented) the following custom among the women of Babylon: "Every woman in the country must once in her life sit down in the temple of Aphrodite (=Ishtar) and have intercourse with a stranger . . . The men pass and make their choice. A woman who has once taken her seat is not allowed to return home until one of the strangers throws a silver coin into her lap and takes her with him beyond the holy ground. When he throws the coin he says these words: 'The goddess Mylitta make you prosper.' (Aphrodite is called Mylitta by the Assyrians.) The silver coin may be of any size; it cannot be refused, for that is forbidden by the law, since once thrown it is sacred. The woman goes with the first man who throws her money, and rejects no one. After their intercourse, she has made herself holy in the sight of the goddess and goes home; and afterward there is no amount of money, however great, that will buy her favors" (*The Histories,* Book I, paragraph 199).

p. 14, *you will see the young men dressed in their splendor* through *in honor of the goddess:* For a literal translation of this passage, see note, p. 213.

p. 16, *She used her love-arts* through *he stayed erect and made love with her*: For a literal translation of this passage, see note, p. 235.

p. 17, *like the fawn that emerges with Alice*: In Chapter 3 of Lewis Carroll's *Through the Looking-Glass*:

> Just then a Fawn came wandering by: it looked at Alice with its large gentle eyes, but didn't seem at all frightened. "Here then! Here then!" Alice said, as she held out her hand and tried to stroke it; but it only started back a little, and then stood looking at her again.
>
> "What do you call yourself?" the Fawn said at last. Such a soft sweet voice it had!
>
> "I wish I knew!" thought poor Alice. She answered, rather sadly, "Nothing, just now."
>
> "Think again," it said: "that won't do."
>
> Alice thought, but nothing came of it. "Please, would you tell me what *you* call yourself?" she said timidly. "I think that might help a little."
>
> "I'll tell you, if you'll move a little further on," the Fawn said. "I can't remember here."
>
> So they walked on together though the wood, Alice with her arms clasped lovingly round the soft neck of the Fawn, till they came out into another open field, and here the Fawn gave a sudden bound into the air, and shook itself free from Alice's arms. "I'm a Fawn!" it cried out in a voice of delight, "and, dear me! you're a human child!" A sudden look of alarm came into its beautiful brown eyes, and in another moment it had darted away at full speed.

p. 17, *"it is not good that the man should be alone"*: Genesis 2:18.

p. 18, *she is gone:* Except for a tantalizing glimpse in the first of the two Old Babylonian tablets in the Schøyen Collection in Norway, OB Schøyen₁, ll. 1′ ff. The text reads (in George's translation, slightly modified): " 'I have acquired a friend, the counselor that I kept seeing in dreams, / Enkidu, the counselor that I kept seeing in dreams.' / Enkidu said to her, to the *harīmtu*: / 'Come, *harīmtu*, let me do you a favor, / because you led me here into Uruk of the Great Square, / because you showed me a fine companion, you showed me a friend.' "

p. 19, *Deep in his heart he felt something stir, / a longing he had never known before, / the longing for a true friend:* For a literal translation of this passage, see note, p. 236.

p. 21, *"The priest will bless the young couple through Gilgamesh, king of great-walled Uruk:* For a literal translation of this passage, see note, p. 239.

p. 21, *It is he who mates first with the lawful wife:* "The interpretation [of this passage] is much debated. It may refer to a normal marriage custom, except that there is no other evidence of Mesopotamian kings having relations with brides before the husbands do. The lines may mean that Gilgamesh's behavior was against custom, and related to his wrongful taking of girls, as the citizens complained in I, 60–64. But how then to reconcile its being 'ordered by the counsel of Anu'? On the other hand, the unique term 'destined wife' . . . suggests that the scene may refer to the ancient cultic practice called by scholars the 'Sacred Marriage,' a ritual act of intercourse originally associated with the coronation rite of the kings in Uruk. In the Ur III and early Old Babylonian periods the cosmic Sacred Marriage of Inanna/Ishtar to Dumuzi/Tammuz was reenacted by their human representatives, a priestess and the king. Could ordinary brides be selected for this role on occasion? If Gilgamesh's behavior is legitimate, is Enkidu's anger due to misunderstanding or to jealousy?" (Kovacs, pp. 16–17).

p. 21, *It is also possible, as some scholars think:* "A third suggestion is that Gilgameš wore his people out with athletic contests. This last idea agrees with the Hittite tradition that Gilgameš triumphed over the young men of Uruk every day, and with the Sumerian poem of Bilgames and the Netherworld. In the latter text it seems that Gilgameš continually engages the young men of Uruk in some kind of time-consuming game or sport involving the *pukku* and *mekkû,* a heavy wooden ball and mallet. The women of Uruk are obliged to spend their days ministering to the needs of their exhausted menfolk until their outcry results in the disappearance of the two objects into the Netherworld" (George, *BGE*, I, p. 449).

p. 23, *as Jacob said to his angel:* Genesis 32:26.

p. 23, *the genital sexuality is explicit:* "According to A. D. Kilmer, the symbols by which Enkidu is represented in the dream episodes make allusion to the Ištar cult: the meteorite, *kiṣru,* evokes *kezru,* who would be a male counterpart of a *kezertu* woman (a kind of cultic prostitute), and the axe, *ḫaṣṣinnu,* evokes *assinnu,* a cultic performer who, typically as a eunuch, took the female role in the sexual act. By this analysis what Gilgameš sees in his dreams is a twofold prediction of the arrival of a close male friend who will also be his lover" (George, *BGE*, I, p. 452). "The repeated use of the verb *ḫabābu* in this connection implies a sexual connection. If there is any doubt about the significance of this imagery, note also SB [Standard Version] VIII 59, where, in death, Gilgameš veils Enkidu 'like a bride.'

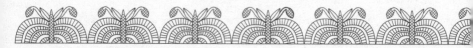

Graphic evidence for a sexual relationship now comes from SB XII
96–9, as understood in the light of a new manuscript of the text's Sumer-
ian forerunner, BN ["Bilgames and the Netherworld"] 250–3" (ibid., p.
454, n. 48). These lines from Tablet XII describe the return of Enkidu's
ghost from the underworld:

> "If I am going to tell you the rules of the Netherworld that I saw,
> sit you down (and) weep!"
> "[(So)] let me sit down and weep!"
> "[My friend, the] penis that you touched so your heart rejoiced,
> grubs devour [(it) . . . like an] old garment.
> [My friend, the crotch that you] touched so your heart rejoiced,
> it is filled with dust [like a crack in the ground.]" (Tablet XII, ll. 93
>   ff., tr. George)

Fascinatingly, the Sumerian text from which this Akkadian text is trans-
lated has Enkidu talking about the decay of a *female* lover of Gilgamesh's:

> "If I am to [tell] you how things are ordered in the Netherworld,
> O sit you down and weep!" "Then I will sit and weep!"
> "The one who handled (your) penis (so) you were glad at heart,
> (and) you said, 'I am going to [. . . *like*] a roof-beam,'
> her vulva is infested with vermin like an [old] cloak,
> her vulva is filled with dust like a crack in the ground."
> ("Bilgamesh and the Netherworld," ll. 248 ff., tr. George)

p. 23, *A boulder representing Enkidu:* Literally, "lump of Anu," i.e., meteorite.

p. 24, *"Thy love to me [is] wonderful, passing the love of women":* 2 Samuel 1:26.

p. 25, *each loves the other as his own soul:* "And when he had finished speaking to Saul, the soul of Jonathan was merged with the soul of David, and Jonathan loved him as his own soul" (1 Samuel 18:1).

p. 26, *ancient Babylonian kings prided themselves:* "The perfect prince was an intellectual as well as a warrior and an athlete, and among his many achievements King Shulgi [2094–2047 BCE] was particularly proud of his literacy and cultural accomplishments. He had rosy memories of his days at the scribal school, where he boasted that he was the most skilled student in his class. In later life he was an enthusiastic patron of the arts and claims to have founded special libraries at Ur and at Nippur, further north in central Babylonia, in which scribes and minstrels could consult master copies of, as it were, the Sumerian songbook. Thus he envisaged that hymns to his glory and other literature of his day would be preserved for posterity:

> For all eternity the Tablet House is never to change,
>> for all eternity the House of Learning is never to cease
>>> functioning." (George, *EG*, xvii)

p. 26, *We must kill him and drive out evil from the world:* The literal text here is fragmentary: "[. . .] kill [. . .], destroy [. . .]." I have adopted the conjecture of Schott (followed by Tournay and Shaffer): "[You and I will] kill [him] / [so that we can] destroy [all the evil in the land]." A later, fragmentary speech, from MS BB₁ col. v, may assign a similar statement to Gilgamesh; in George's restoration, it reads: "[During the days that we travel there and] back, / [until we reach the Forest of] Cedar, / [until we] slay [ferocious Humbaba,] / [and annihilate] from [the land the Evil Thing that Šamaš hates]" (Standard Version III, 202 ff.).

p. 27, *the poet does provide a motivation:* This motivation is at least as old as the Sumerian poem "Gilgamesh and Huwawa" (Version A), ll. 28 ff.: "No one is tall enough to reach heaven; no one can reach wide enough to stretch over the mountains. Since a man cannot pass beyond the final end of life, I want to set off into the mountains, to establish my renown there. Where renown can be established there, I will establish my renown" (from the translation posted on the Sumerian Literature site of the Oriental Institute, University of Oxford, at http://www-etcsl.orient.ox.ac.uk/cgi-bin/etcslmac.cgi?text=t.1.8.1.2#). It is also found in the Old Babylonian Yale tablet, OB III, l. 188: "I will establish an everlasting name."

p. 27, *can produce great art:*

> *Fame* is the spur that the clear spirit doth raise
> (That last infirmity of Noble mind)
> To scorn delights, and live laborious dayes.
> (Milton, "Lycidas," ll. 70–72)

p. 29, *the cause of all human misery:* "I have discovered that all human misery comes from a single thing, the inability to sit at peace in a room" (Blaise Pascal, *Pensées,* fragment 139).

p. 30, *hasn't harmed a single living being:* When attacked, Humbaba does *threaten* to kill Gilgamesh and Enkidu. (There is even a hint of cannibalism—"I didn't kill you, you were too scrawny, / you wouldn't have made a decent meal"—though this line is actually difficult to decipher; George translates it as "[. . .] . . . you, . . . in my belly.") But these threats are not actions; they are words to terrify men away from the forest.

p. 30, *"If anyone knows the rules of my forest:* For a literal translation of this passage, see note, p. 256.

p. 31, *to paraphrase Wallace Stevens:* "If there must be a god in the house . . ." ("Less and Less Human, O Savage Spirit," *The Collected Poems of Wallace Stevens,* Knopf, 1954, p. 327).

p. 31, *Seng-ts'an:* Seng-ts'an (?–606) was a Chinese monk and the Third Founding Teacher of Zen. This couplet is from his poem "The Mind of Absolute Trust," in Stephen Mitchell, ed., *The Enlightened Heart: An Anthology of Sacred Poetry,* HarperCollins, 1989, p. 26.

p. 32, *one fragmentary passage:* See note, p. 232.

p. 32, *by the method known as "reversal of values":* "All these dreams are terrifying; but they are always interpreted by the method known as 'reversal of values': the evil seen in the dream is turned around, in the future reality, into something favorable" (Bottéro, p. 100).

p. 33, *imperviously brave men:* Siegfried is "a man who doesn't know the meaning of fear." As for Beowulf, he is portrayed as fearless in the battles with Grendel and with Grendel's mother ("he didn't fear at all for his life," l. 1444), and in the battle with the dragon, he feels "no dread at all" (l. 2348). It is true that later in the battle he and the dragon are said to cause "terror in each other" (l. 2565). And yet, what Beowulf seems to be feeling at that moment is not what we would call fear. He is in a state of rage, totally focused on killing his enemy. His adrenaline is telling him not to flee but to attack. In the very next line, he is described as "unyielding" ("firm-spirited"

in another translation, "stout" in another). So whatever the poet means by "terror," it is not the same kind of emotion described in *Gilgamesh,* where the heroes feel despair, their blood runs cold, and they want to run away.

p. 33, *his predecessor in the Sumerian poem "Gilgamesh and Huwawa,":* In "Gilgamesh and Huwawa" (Version A). Here is that poem's climax (in the translation from the Sumerian Literature site of the Oriental Institute, University of Oxford, ll. 152G ff.):

> Huwawa sat down and began to weep, shedding tears. Huwawa . . . plea . . . to Gilgamesh. He tugged at Gilgamesh's hand. "I want to talk to Utu! (=Shamash—S. M.)" "Utu, I never knew a mother who bore me, nor a father who brought me up! I was born in the mountains—you brought me up! Yet Gilgamesh swore to me by heaven, by earth, and by the mountains."
>
> Huwawa clutched at Gilgamesh's hand, and prostrated himself before him. Then Gilgamesh's noble heart took pity on him. Gilgamesh addressed Enkidu: "Enkidu, let the captured bird run away home! Let the captured man return to his mother's embrace!"
>
> Enkidu replied to Gilgamesh: "Come on now, you heroic bearer of a sceptre of wide-ranging power! Noble glory of the gods, angry bull standing ready for a fight! Young lord Gilgamesh, cherished in Unug, your mother knew well how to bear sons, and your nurse knew well how to nourish children!—One so exalted and yet so lacking in understanding will be devoured by fate without him ever understanding that fate. The very idea that a captured bird should run away home, or a captured man should return to his mother's embrace!—Then you yourself would never get back to the mother-city that bore you!"

Huwawa addressed Enkidu: "Enkidu, you speak such hateful words against me to him! You hireling, who are hired for your keep! You who follow along after him—why do you speak such hateful words to him?"

As Huwawa spoke thus to him, Enkidu, full of rage and anger, cut his throat. He put his head in a leather bag.

They entered before Enlil. After they had kissed the ground before Enlil, they threw the leather bag down, tipped out his head, and placed it before Enlil. When Enlil saw the head of Huwawa, he spoke angrily to Gilgamesh: "Why did you act in this way? He should have sat before you! He should have eaten the bread that you eat, and should have drunk the water that you drink! He should have been honoured . . . you!"

p. 34, *he is aware that killing him:* "For a reason that is unclear to us, but without doubt primarily because of the 'divine' character of Humbaba and of the mission that the king of the gods had assigned to him . . . , Enlil did not want the Guardian of the Forest to be killed, and Enkidu knew it. Hence his eagerness to put him to death before Enlil could intervene from his great temple in Nippur, and Šamaš from his, in Larsa or Sippar. Šamaš was thus thought to be opposed to the death of the adversary of his two protégés: in other words, he was willing to help them defeat Humbaba, in order to use him as they wished, with his forest and especially his cedars, but not to destroy him. The rest of the story follows from this fact: Enkidu, held responsible for the death of Humbaba, will be condemned by the gods to a premature end" (Bottéro, p. 117).

p. 35, *"played a greater role in myth, epic, and hymn:* Samuel Noah Kramer, *From the Poetry of Sumer: Creation, Glorification, Adoration,* University of California Press, 1979, p. 71.

pp. 35–36, *marvelously erotic song cycle:* I am referring to the versions by Diane Wolkstein in *Inanna, Queen of Heaven and Earth: Her Stories and Hymns from Sumer* (with Samuel Noah Kramer), Harper & Row, 1983. Some of the most delicious of them are reprinted in Robert Hass and Stephen Mitchell, ed., *Into the Garden: A Wedding Anthology,* HarperCollins, 1993.

p. 36, *an invocation to the "goddess...":* "Goddess of the fearsome divine powers, clad in terror, riding on the great divine powers, Inanna, made complete by the strength of the holy *ankar* weapon, drenched in blood, rushing around in great battles, with shield resting on the ground (?), covered in storm and flood, great lady Inanna, knowing well how to plan conflicts, you destroy mighty lands with arrow and strength and overpower lands" (from the translation posted at http://www.gatewaystobabylon.com/myths/texts/inanna/inannaebih.htm#top).

p. 36, *first the Sumerians:* The Sumerian poem "Gilgamesh and the Bull of Heaven," though it is without an equivalent to Gilgamesh's long diatribe, has basically the same plot: it begins with Gilgamesh's rejection of the goddess's advances and ends with him flinging a haunch of the slaughtered Bull at her.

p. 36 *later compared to dogs and flies:* In Book XI, pp. 186, 188.

p. 38, *the roughly contemporaneous bull-leaping fresco:* Painted ca. 1600 to 1400 BCE, the time of the Old Babylonian version. A photograph of the fresco can be found on http://www.daedalus.gr/DAEI/THEME/B30.jpg and on many other Internet websites.

p. 41, *the killing of Humbaba will have fatal consequences:* The explicit causality of Enkidu's death is missing from the Standard Version, and most translators fill in with a passage from the Hittite version: literally, "I dreamed that Anu, Enlil, and Shamash held a council, and Anu said to Enlil, 'Because they killed the Bull of Heaven and also killed Humbaba, one of them must die.' Then Enlil said to him, 'Enkidu, not Gilgamesh, is the one who must die.' " (Tablet III, §1, ll. 2 ff.)

It is impossible to know whether in the Standard Version Anu as well as Enlil is involved in the death sentence, and whether Enkidu is condemned for killing both monsters or only Humbaba.

p. 44, *like a woman who has lost her only child:* For a literal translation of this line, see note, p. 268.

p. 46, *"When you see the unborn:* Here is a more literal version of the Buddha's statement: "There is an unborn, unoriginated, uncreated, unformed. If there were not this unborn, unoriginated, uncreated, unformed, escape from what is born, originated, created, and formed would not be possible. But since there is an unborn, unoriginated, uncreated, unformed, escape is possible from what is born, originated, created, and formed." (Udana 8.3).

p. 46, *"the epic of the fear of death":* See note, p. 202.

p. 48, *Abu Yazid al-Bistami:* Stephen Mitchell, ed., *The Enlightened Mind: An Anthology of Sacred Prose,* HarperCollins, 1991, p. 76.

p. 49, *Shiduri:* "This character is mysterious, and otherwise unknown. She is a married woman, as is indicated by the 'veil' that she wears; and she belongs to the supernatural world, since her name is preceded, in cuneiform, by the sign that indicates a god. She is a 'tavern keeper': that is, according to a custom current until the second half of the second millennium (afterward, the role was taken over by men), she runs a sort of bar in which she sells to the public beer—the country's national drink—that she has made (her professional apparatus is mentioned in verse 3). Besides being a drinking establishment, the tavern also represented the 'commerce of the crossroads,' where many commodities of primary necessity were sold, and whose managers were better qualified than anyone else to give information, not only about their clientele, but also about the country. Shiduri is the model, projected into legend, of these 'business people of the crossroads,' even if it's difficult to see who her clients could be, here at the edge of the world . . . The author needed her as a figure who could give information to Gilgameš, and folklore can do without logic" (Bottéro, p. 165).

p. 52, *the same questions Shiduri asked:* Urshanabi asks them as well, but I have omitted that part of the dialogue between him and Gilgamesh.

p. 52, *Tell us how not to believe what we think:* See Byron Katie, with Stephen Mitchell, *Loving What Is: Four Questions That Can Change Your Life,* Harmony Books, 2002.

p. 53, *for St. Paul to tell the Thessalonians that they were* not *going to die:* Paul believed that the "second coming" would happen during his lifetime. "For the Lord himself will descend from heaven with a shout, with the archangel's call, and with the trumpet of God. And the dead in Christ will rise first, then we who are alive and are left will be caught up together with them in the clouds, to meet the Lord in the air" (1 Thessalonians 4:16–17).

p. 53, *tells him about the Great Flood:* His speech has been adapted from an older poem called *Atrahasis.* Most scholars (e.g., Tigay, pp. 238 ff.) think that the adaptor was Sîn-lēqi-unninni, but since no fragments of the Old Babylonian version of Book XI have survived, we don't know whether it too contained the long Flood story.

p. 54, *clustering around it like flies:* This image, unlike many of the others, was borrowed from the *Atrahasis.*

p. 54, *abridge the Flood story:* Here is one way it might be abridged:

> "You know Shuruppak, that ancient city.
> I was its king once, long ago,
> when the great gods decided to send the Flood.
> Ea informed me, and I built a large ship.
> I loaded onto her everything precious
> that I owned. Very soon the Flood burst forth.
> For six days and seven nights, the storm
> demolished the earth. On the seventh day,
> the downpour stopped. The ocean grew calm.
> No land could be seen. There was no life at all.
> The human race had turned into clay.

When the waters had dried up and land appeared,
the gods assembled. Enlil blessed us,
me and my wife. 'You gods, from now on
Utnapishtim and his wife shall be
gods like us, they shall live forever.'
Then they brought us to this distant place
at the source of the rivers. Here we live."

p. 55, *to experience all that terror, and the death of almost every living thing:* Utnapish-
tim's compassion and sorrow for the people left behind are more explicit
in the *Atrahasis:* "He invited his people […] / […] to a feast. / […] he
put his family on board. / They were eating, they were drinking, / But he
went in and out, / Could not stay still or rest on his haunches, / His heart
was breaking and he was vomiting bile" (Dalley, p. 31).

p. 56, *the "unsleeping, undying" gods:* From Utnapishtim's speech:

"At night the moon travels across the sky,
the gods of heaven stay awake and watch us,
unsleeping, undying. This is the way
the world is established, from ancient times."

p. 56, *"an animal [or a god] can't know":* From Book I:

He [Enkidu] turned back to Shamhat, and as he walked
he knew that his mind had somehow grown larger,
he knew things now that an animal can't know.

p. 59, *"At four hundred miles they stopped to eat, / at a thousand miles they pitched their camp"*: See note, p. 283.

p. 60, *"satisfied with good things"* . . . *"youth is renewed like the eagle's"*: Psalm 103:5.

p. 63, *managed to "close the gate of sorrow"*: From the conclusion of Gilgamesh's first long speech to Utnapishtim in Book X:

> "Now let
> the gate of sorrow be closed behind me,
> and let it be sealed shut with tar and pitch."

p. 63, *"When I argue with reality, I lose"*: Byron Katie, *Loving What Is*, p. 2.

ABOUT THIS VERSION

p. 65, *literal translations:* For the complexities of decipherment and translation, see George, *EG*, pp. 209 ff.

p. 66, *"Sestina"*: Elizabeth Bishop, *The Complete Poems, 1927–1979*, Farrar, Straus and Giroux, 1983, pp. 123–24.

PROLOGUE

p. 69, *He had seen everything:* Literally, "He who saw the Deep" or "He who saw everything" (in Akkadian, *Sha naqba imuru*). The poem's first line also served as its title. "The word *naqbu* has two meanings, (a) 'totality' and (b) the deep body of underground water believed to supply springs and

wells, that is, the cosmic realm of Ea better known as the Apsû" (George, *BGE*, I, p. 444).

p. 69, *had restored the holy Eanna Temple and the massive / wall of Uruk:* Literally, "had built the wall of Uruk-of-the-Sheepfold and the sacred storehouse of holy Eanna." Here Sîn-lēqi-unninni seems to say, by the sequence of actions, that Gilgamesh built the wall and the Eanna Temple *after* he returned from his journey to Utnapishtim. But of course the wall and the temple are very much present during the action of the poem, and Gilgamesh proudly points out the wall to Urshanabi on their return. In fact, the next line asserts that the wall was founded by the Seven Sages long before the Flood. (Literally, "Isn't its masonry made of kiln-fired brick, and didn't the Seven Sages themselves lay its foundations?" The Seven Sages were antediluvian kings who, themselves taught by the god Ea, had taught humanity all the arts of civilization.) Obviously there were other builders of the wall, though Gilgamesh was considered the most famous. So I have said "restored" rather than "built."

p. 69, *gleam like copper:* Following Kovacs.

p. 70, *observe the land it encloses: the palm trees, the gardens, / the orchards, the glorious palaces and temples, the shops / and marketplaces, the houses, the public squares:* Literally, "One šār (1½ square miles) is city, one šār palm gardens, one šār clay-pits, half a šār the Ishtar Temple—Uruk measures three and a half šār."

BOOK I

p. 71, *Surpassing all kings* (in Akkadian, *Shūtur eli sharri*): The first line of the Old Babylonian version, and its title.

p. 71, *two-thirds divine and one-third human:* My friend Philip Ording points out that this is as mathematically impossible as being two-thirds English and one-third French. I have moved the line forward; it occurs a bit later in Tablet I.

p. 72, *he brought back the ancient, forgotten rites, / restoring the temples that the Flood had destroyed, / renewing the statutes and sacraments / for the welfare of the people and the sacred land:* Literally, "he restored the sanctuaries that the Flood had destroyed and reestablished the rituals for the human race." I have added a few clarifying phrases from the Sumerian poem "The Death of Gilgamesh" (version from Me-Turan, segment F, ll. 14 ff.). Literally, "establishing temples of the gods, reaching Ziusudra (=Utnapishtim) in his abode, reestablishing the rites of Sumer, forgotten since ancient times, the ordinances and rituals, you carried out the rites of purification, you understood everything that was needful for the land, from before the Flood."

p. 72, *The goddess Aruru, mother of creation, / had designed his body, had made him the strongest / of men—huge, handsome, radiant, perfect:* Literally, "Bēlet-ilī (=Aruru) drew the image of his body, Nudimmud (=Ea) brought his form to perfection. [. . .] was majestic [. . .] stature [. . .]." I have omitted a brief fragmentary description of Gilgamesh as a giant: "His feet were 3 cubits (4½ feet) long, his legs 6 cubits (9 feet) tall, his stride 6 cubits, his thumb was [. . .] cubits, his cheeks were bearded like [. . .], the hairs of his head were as thick as barley." According to the later Hittite version, he was 11 cubits, or more than 16½ feet, tall. (Interestingly enough, this is about the height of the magnificent human-headed winged bull from the throne room of Sargon II in Khorsabad, now at the Oriental Institute in Chicago, http://www-oi.uchicago.edu/OI /MUS/HIGH/OIM_A7369_72dpi.html.) By contrast, Goliath was 6 cubits and a span (9¾ feet) tall (1 Samuel 17:4).

p. 72 *takes the son from his father and crushes him:* The nature of this oppression is unclear; it may be some kind of forced labor or military service.

p. 73, *But the people of Uruk cried out to heaven, / and their lamentation was heard, the gods / are not unfeeling, their hearts were touched, / they went to Anu, father of them all, / protector of the realm of sacred Uruk, / and spoke to him on the people's behalf: / "Heavenly Father, Gilgamesh— / noble as he is, splendid as he is— / has exceeded all bounds. The people suffer / from his tyranny, the people cry out / that he takes the son from his father and crushes him, / takes the girl from her mother and uses her, / the warrior's daughter, the young man's bride, / he uses her, no one dares to oppose him. / Is this how you want your king to rule? / Should a shepherd savage his own flock? Father, / do something, quickly, before the people / overwhelm heaven with their heartrending cries.":* Literally, "[The women (George's conjecture)] their [. . .] soon, [. . .] complaint [. . .] before [them]: 'Powerful, preeminent, expert, [. . .] Gilgamesh does not leave a girl to [her bridegroom], the warrior's daughter, the young man's bride.' The goddesses kept hearing their complaints. The gods of heaven, the lords who command, [to Anu], 'You have created an arrogant wild bull in Uruk-the-Sheepfold, he has no equal who can raise a weapon [against him], his companions are always ready to obey his orders (*or* are kept on their feet by the ball), he oppresses [the young men of Uruk], he does not leave a son to his father, day and [night his violence grows] worse. Yet he is the shepherd of Uruk-the-Sheepfold, Gilgamesh, [who guides the] teeming [people], he is their shepherd and their [. . .], powerful, preeminent, expert, [. . .]. Gilgamesh does not leave a girl to her bride[groom]—the warrior's daughter, the young [man's] bride.' "

p. 74, *Anu heard them, he nodded his head,* / *then to the goddess, mother of creation,* / *he called out: "Aruru, you are the one* / *who created humans. Now go and create* / *a double for Gilgamesh, his second self,* / *a man who equals his strength and courage,* / *a man who equals his stormy heart.* / *Create a new hero, let them balance each other* / *perfectly,* *so that Uruk has peace.":* Literally, "[Anu] listened to their complaints. They summoned the great goddess Aruru: 'Aruru, you are the one who created [mankind], now create one like him. Let him be equal to his stormy heart, let them be a match for each other so that Uruk has peace.' "

p. 75, *a trapper:* "The word is commonly translated 'hunter,' but 'trapper' seems more accurate here because the animals are captured in traps or pits, not killed by weapons" (Kovacs, p. 6).

p. 76, *then follow his advice. He will know what to do:* I have omitted the father's specific instructions about Shamhat, which are repeated word for word in Gilgamesh's speech. I have also omitted, in the trapper's speech to Gilgamesh, the description of Enkidu, repeated word for word from his speech to his father.

pp. 76–77, *"Go to the temple of Ishtar,* / *ask them there for a woman named Shamhat,* / *one of the priestesses who give their bodies* / *to any man, in honor of the goddess.* / *Take*

her into the wilderness. / When the animals are drinking at the waterhole, / tell her to strip off her robe and lie there / naked, ready, with her legs apart. / The wild man will approach. Let her use her love-arts. / Nature will take its course, and then / the animals who knew him in the wilderness / will be bewildered, and will leave him forever: Literally, "Go, trapper, take Shamhat, the *ḫarīmtu*, with you. When the animals are drinking at the waterhole, have her take off her robe and expose her vagina. When he sees her he will approach, and his animals will be estranged from him, though he grew up in their presence."

p. 78, *They looked in amazement. The man was huge / and beautiful. Deep in Shamhat's loins / desire stirred. Her breath quickened / as she stared at this primordial being:* Literally, "Shamhat saw him—the primeval man, the savage from the midst of the wilderness."

p. 78, *Stir up his lust when he approaches, / touch him, excite him, take his breath / with your kisses, show him what a woman is:* Literally, "Don't hold back, take his vital force. When he sees you he will approach you. Spread out your robe, let him lie on top of you, and stir up his lust, the work of a woman."

pp. 78–79, *She stripped off her robe and lay there naked, / with her legs apart, touching herself. / Enkidu saw her and warily approached. / He sniffed the air. He gazed at her body. / He drew close, Shamhat touched him on the thigh, / touched his penis, and put him inside her. / She used her love-arts, she took his breath / with her kisses, held nothing back, and showed him / what a woman is. For seven days / he stayed erect and made love with her, / until he had had enough:* Literally, "She took off her robe, she exposed her vagina, and he took in her voluptuousness. She didn't hold back, she took his vital force. She spread out her robe and let him lie upon her, she stirred up his lust, the work of a woman. With passion he embraced and caressed her, for six days and seven nights Enkidu

remained erect, he made love with her until he had had enough of her delights."

p. 80, "*Now, Enkidu, you know what it is / to be with a woman, to unite with her. / You are beautiful, you are like a god:* Literally, "You are handsome, Enkidu, you are like a god." The context seems to indicate understanding rather than beauty. One can't help comparing the words of the serpent in the Garden of Eden: "as soon as you eat from it, your eyes will be opened, and you will be like gods, knowing good and evil" (Genesis 3:5).

p. 80, *She finished, and Enkidu nodded his head. / Deep in his heart he felt something stir, / a longing he had never known before, / the longing for a true friend:* Literally, "She spoke, and her words found favor. He became aware that he was longing for a friend."

p. 81, *"Come," said Shamhat, "let us go to Uruk, / I will lead you to Gilgamesh the mighty king. / You will see the great city with its massive wall, / you will see the young men dressed in their splendor, / in the finest linen and embroidered wool, / brilliantly colored, with fringed shawls and wide belts:* Literally, "Let [him] see your face, [I will lead you to Gilgamesh,] I know where he will be. Come, Enkidu, to Uruk-the-Sheepfold, where the young men are girt with waistbands." I have taken the details of the young men's clothing from R. Turner Wilcox, *The Mode in Costume,* Macmillan, 2nd edition, 1983; see http://www.geocities.com/FashionAvenue/3105/costume1.html and http://handsofchange.org/costume.html. "The costumes of the Babylonians and the Assyrians consisted of two garments, a straight tunic edged with fringe, either long or short, called the candys, and a fringed shawl of varying dimensions. . . . The addition of a wide belt worn about the waist was common. . . . Linen was used, but the principal fabric seems to have been wool, elaborately embroidered with separate motifs founded upon the design of the rosette. . . . Garments were always trimmed with fringe and tassels. [The Babylonians] were fond of brilliant colors in reds, greens, blues, and purples."

p. 81, *Every day is a festival in Uruk, / with people singing and dancing in the streets, / musicians playing their lyres and drums, / the lovely priestesses standing before / the temple of Ishtar, chatting and laughing, / flushed with sexual joy, and ready / to serve men's pleasure, in honor of the goddess:* Literally, "Every day [. . .] a festival is held, the lyre and drum are played, the *ḫarimāti* stand around, lovely, laughing, filled with sexual joy." Gardner translates this last line "radiating sexual prowess, filled with sex-joy," and his coauthor John Maier explains, "The sexual prowess is *kuzbu*; sex-joy is *rišatum*. 'Beauty' and *kuzbu* are not restricted at all to women; both are attributes of Gilgamesh and of gods as well as goddesses" (Maier, in Gardner and Maier, pp. 81 ff.).

p. 82, *Shamash, the sun god:* "Šamaš was said to have surrounded with his particular protection not only Gilgameš but his whole dynasty, the founder of which, Meskiaggašer, was 'Šamaš's son,' according to the Sumerian List of Kings. We find in this passage, as very often throughout the poem, the great triad of supreme gods who in Mesopotamia presided over the pantheon and the universe: An or Anu, god of the sky and father and founder of the reigning divine dynasty; Enlil, god of the earth, sovereign of the gods and of men; and Ea or Enki, the most intelligent of the gods, creator of men and of civilization" (Bottéro, p. 78).

p. 82, *you had come to Gilgamesh in a dream." / And she told Enkidu what she had heard. / "He went to his mother, the goddess Ninsun:* Literally, " 'Gilgamesh in Uruk dreamed about you.' Gilgamesh went to reveal the dream, saying to his mother." Following Ferry, I have omitted a second dream and interpretation, which is almost exactly like the first one.

pp. 83–84, *it stands for a dear friend, a mighty hero. / You will take him in your arms, embrace and caress him / the way a man caresses his wife. / He will be your double, your second self, / a man who is loyal, who will stand at your side / through the greatest dangers. Soon you will meet him, / the companion of your heart. Your dream has said so:* Literally, "This means that a strong man will come to you, someone who will rescue his friend. He is the mightiest in the land, he has strength, his strength is as powerful as a meteorite from the sky. You will love him like a wife, caressing and embracing him. He will be strong and will rescue you again and again. Your dream is excellent and favorable."

BOOK II

p. 85, *Then Shamhat gave Enkidu one of her robes / and he put it on:* From OB II, ll. 69–70.

p. 85, *she led him like a child:* Literally, "she led him as a god [leads a suppliant]." "This refers to so-called 'presentation scenes' depicted on cylinder-seals, which show a god leading the owner of the seal by the hand into the presence of a more powerful god" (Bottéro, p. 83). George has a different interpretation; see *BGE* I, p. 167.

pp. 85–86, *He had never seen human food* through *Enkidu went out with sword and spear:* From OB II, ll. 90 ff.

pp. 85–86, *"Go ahead, Enkidu. This is food, / we humans eat and drink this." Warily / he tasted the bread. Then he ate a piece, / he ate a whole loaf, then ate another, / he ate until he was full:* Literally, " 'Eat the bread, Enkidu, the staff of life, drink the beer, the custom of the land.' Enkidu ate the bread until he was full."

pp. 86–88, *One day, while he was making love* through *the guests were eating, singing and laughing:* From OB II, ll. 135 ff. (except for "like a little baby they kissed his feet," which is from the Standard Version).

p. 87, *The priest will bless the young couple, the guests / will rejoice, the bridegroom will step aside, / and the virgin will wait in the marriage bed / for Gilgamesh, king of great-walled Uruk:* Literally, "For the king of Uruk of the Great Square, the (fence: Tournay and Shaffer; veil: George) will open for (the people to choose [a bride]: Tournay and Shaffer; the one who has first pick: George)"; the two verses are repeated with a slight variation.

pp. 87–88, *"I will go to Uruk now, / to the palace of Gilgamesh the mighty king. / I will challenge him. I will shout to his face: / 'I am the mightiest! I am the man / who can make the world tremble! I am supreme!'"* // *Together they went to great-walled Uruk:* There is a gap in the text here, and I have filled it in by repeating Enkidu's earlier speech.

p. 88, *Gilgamesh truly has met his match. / This wild man can rival the mightiest of kings:* I have added these lines.

pp. 88–90, *The wedding ritual had taken place* through *you are destined to rule over men:* From OB II, ll. 190 ff. The phrases "With his feet Enkidu blocked the door (to the wedding house) and didn't allow Gilgamesh to enter," "they seized each other (in the doorway of the wedding house)," and "the doorposts trembled, the walls shook" also appear in the equivalent, abbreviated passage from the Standard Version.

pp. 88–89, *The wedding ritual had taken place, / the musicians were playing their drums and lyres, / the guests were eating, singing and laughing, / the bride was ready for Gilgamesh / as though for a god, she was waiting in her bed / to open to him, in honor of Ishtar, / to forget her husband and open to the king:* Literally, "In Uruk the sacrifice was being performed, the young men were celebrating for the hero [?]. For the handsome young man, for Gilgamesh, the partner was made ready as for a god, the bed was made for the goddess Ishara (=Ishtar), so that Gilgamesh could join with the bride that night." George interprets the passage differently; see *BGE*, I, pp. 169–70, 190, 455–56.

p. 89, *When Gilgamesh reached the marriage house, / Enkidu was there. He stood like a boulder, / blocking the door. Gilgamesh, raging, / stepped up and seized him, huge arms gripped / huge arms, foreheads crashed like wild bulls, / the two men staggered, they pitched against houses, / the doorposts trembled, the outer walls shook, / they careened through the streets, they grappled each other, / limbs intertwined, each huge body / straining to break free from the other's embrace:* Literally, "He came forward and stood in the street, he blocked Gilgamesh's path. [*gap*] [. . .] In front of him [. . .] he was getting angry [. . .] Enkidu moved toward him, they faced each other in the great square. With his feet Enkidu blocked the door, he didn't allow Gilgamesh to enter. They seized each other, bending their backs like bulls, they shattered the doorposts, the walls shook. Gilgamesh and Enkidu seized each other, bending their backs like bulls, they shattered the doorposts, the walls shook."

p. 89, *Finally, Gilgamesh threw the wild man / and with his right knee pinned him to the ground:* Literally, "Gilgamesh knelt, his foot on the ground."

p. 90, *They embraced and kissed. They held hands like brothers. / They walked side by side. They became true friends:* From OB III, l. 18. Literally, "They kissed each other and formed a friendship." The Standard Version continues with a fragmentary dialogue between Ninsun and Gilgamesh, which I have omitted.

BOOK III

p. 91, *Time passed quickly:* I have added this phrase and have begun Book III with the following passage from the Yale tablet (OB III) because there is a natural break in the story at this point. Tablet III begins with the following lines: "Come back safely to the haven of Uruk; do not trust in your strength alone."

p. 91, *Gilgamesh said, / "Now we must travel to the Cedar Forest, / where the fierce monster Humbaba lives. / We must kill him and drive out evil from the world.":* This fragmentary passage is from OB III, ll. 89–90, 97 ff. Literally, "Gilgamesh opened his mouth, saying to Enkidu, [*gap*] 'fierce Huwawa (=Humbaba). [. . .] kill him, destroy [. . .].' " I have adopted Schott's conjecture: "[You and I will] kill [him] / [so that we can] destroy [all the evil in the land]."

p. 91, *Cedar Forest:* As opposed to the Sumerian poem "Gilgamesh and Huwawa," in which the Cedar Forest lies to the east, in southwestern Iran, the Standard Version locates it to the west, in what is now Syria.

p. 91, *Enkidu sighed. His eyes filled with tears* through *sticks in my throat, my arms are limp:* I have taken these lines from a fragmentary passage omitted here, in which Gilgamesh introduces Enkidu to his mother, the goddess Ninsun.

pp. 91–92, *I knew that country when I roamed the hills* through *I have to enter it, climb its slopes:* From OB III, ll. 106 ff. I have left out a few lines that are repeated in the Standard Version.

p. 91, *it spreads far and wide for a thousand miles:* Literally, "The forest extends for 60 *bēr* in every direction." Sixty *bēr* or double leagues = 648 kilometers or about 400 miles. The expression really means "a large (indeterminate) number of miles," which in a base-10 number system like ours (the Mesopotamians' system was based on 60) would be 100 or 1,000 miles.

p. 92, *cut down a cedar that is tall enough / to make a whirlwind as it falls to earth:* Following Foster's restoration.

p. 92, *cut down a cedar:* "The cedar was the luxury wood par excellence—fragrant, solid, tall, and fine-grained—for the richest public buildings, palaces, and temples" (Bottéro, p. 123).

pp. 93–94, *We are not gods, we cannot ascend* through *I will stamp my fame on men's minds forever:* From OB III, ll. 140 ff., except for "You are brave, your heart has been tested in combat," which is from the Standard Version.

p. 93, *If I die in the forest on this great adventure, / won't you be ashamed when people say, / 'Gilgamesh met a hero's death / battling the monster Humbaba. And where / was Enkidu? He was safe at home!':* Literally, "I will go in front of you, and you can call out, 'Go on, don't be afraid!' If I die, I will have established my fame. [People will say,] 'Gilgamesh battled with the fierce Humbaba.' "

p. 94, *But whether you come along or not, / I will cut down the tree, I will kill Humbaba, / I will make a lasting name for myself, / I will stamp my fame on men's minds forever":* Literally, "I must start work and cut down the cedar, I must establish my everlasting fame."

pp. 94–95, *Gilgamesh bolted the seven gates* through *I will stamp my fame on men's minds forever:* From OB III, ll. 172 ff. I have moved the episode with the smiths to later in Book III.

p. 95, *celebrate the New Year:* "One of the greatest festivals of the annual liturgy: the *akîtu,* for the ceremonies of which a particular sanctuary outside the city walls was reserved, to which the people walked in procession from the city" (Bottéro, p. 90).

p. 96, *he is horrible to look at:* "The 'mask of Huwawa/Humbaba,' grimacing and hideous, was well known, and often reproduced as an amulet" (Bottéro, p. 91).

p. 97, *After he had listened to the elders' words, / Gilgamesh laughed. He got up and said, / "Dear friend, tell me, has your courage returned? / Are you ready to leave? Or are you still / afraid of dying a hero's death?*: From OB III, ll. 201 ff. Literally, "He looked at Enkidu and laughed. 'Now, my friend [. . .] Should I be so afraid of him that I [. . .]." I have omitted a speech of the elders that is repeated word for word later in Tablet III and have inserted the visit to the foundry here.

pp. 97–98, *Enkidu, let us go to the forge* through *weighing more than six hundred pounds*: From OB III, ll. 161 ff.

p. 97, *and order the smiths to make us weapons / that only the mightiest heroes could use." // Enkidu listened gravely. He stood / silent there for a long time. At last / he nodded. Gilgamesh took his hand*: Literally, " 'Let them cast [whatever axes] we will need.' They took [each other by the hand] and went to the forge."

p. 98, *two hundred pounds*: Literally, "3 talents" = 87 kg. = 191 lbs.

p. 98, *six hundred pounds*: Literally, "10 talents."

p. 98, *Gilgamesh said, "Before we leave*: I have omitted a speech that begins "The elders stood up and addressed the king: / 'Come back safely . . . '" It is repeated word for word later in Book III.

p. 99, *Dear mother, great goddess, help me in this*: I have added this line and omitted the last three lines of Gilgamesh's speech, which, like the rest of the passage, are repeated word for word from the address to the young men.

p. 99, *soapwort*: "This is the plant *tullal*; it has not been identified, but its name (it means, in Akkadian, 'You purify') indicates its usage, in both personal hygiene and the operations of 'magic' and exorcism, as a detergent. Ninsun, by 'purifying' herself, puts herself in a condition to address Šamaš, a god of higher rank than she" (Bottéro, p. 94).

p. 99, *went up to the roof*: "In this hot country, in which rain is quite rare, the roofs were, and still are, entirely flat, and serve as terraces" (Bottéro, p. 192).

p. 99, *"Lord of heaven, you have granted my son / beauty and strength and courage*: I have added these lines.

p. 100, *O Lord Shamash, glorious sun, / delight of the gods, illuminator / of the world, who rise and the light is born, / it fills the heavens, the whole earth takes shape, / the mountains form, the valleys grow bright, / darkness vanishes, evil retreats, / all creatures wake up and open their eyes, / they see you, they are filled with joy— / protect my son. On his dangerous journey*: Literally, "O [Shamash], you opened [. . .] for the animals of the wilderness, you came out for the land to [. . .], the mountains [. . .], the heavens grow [bright], animals of the wilderness [. . .] your radiance. [. . .] waited for [. . .] them, the animals [. . .] you. [. . .] I am offering you, the dead man [. . .] life. To the [. . .] your head, when [your light] rises crowds assemble, the great gods wait for [your light], [may Aya your bride] not be afraid [to remind you]: [Entrust] him to [the watchmen of the night]. The road that [. . .] touch and [. . .]. Because [. . .] the journey [. . .] And [. . .] while Gilgamesh travels to the Cedar [Forest]."

p. 101, *stir up strong winds:* The Standard Version specifies thirteen winds. Because there are so few relatively synonymous nouns for "wind" in English, I have reduced the number to eight, as in the Hittite version.

p. 101, *After she had prayed:* I have omitted the following passage, which comes from a different strand of the tradition and whose irony seems an unfruitful contrast with Gilgamesh's awareness that "we are not gods, we are mortal men": "Ninsun made a second prayer to Shamash: 'O Shamash, won't Gilgamesh [. . .] the gods? Won't he share the heavens with you? Won't he share a scepter with the moon? Won't he act in wisdom with Ea in the Great Deep? Won't he rule the black-headed race with Irnina (=Ishtar)? Won't he dwell with Ningishzida in the Land of No Return?' "

p. 102, *Enkidu listened. Tears filled his eyes.* / *He and Gilgamesh clasped hands like brothers.* // *They took their weapons: the massive axes,* / *the massive knives, the quivers, the bows:* There is a large gap in the text here. I have omitted three fragmentary passages and added these lines.

p. 102, *Remember what the ancient proverb says:* I have added this line.

p. 103, *May Shamash grant you your heart's desire* through *and remember Lugalbanda your father:* From OB III, ll. 257 ff.

p. 103, *who journeyed to far-off mountains himself:* I have followed a hint in one of Kovacs's footnotes and added this line. In two Sumerian poems, "Lugalbanda and Enmerkar" and "Lugalbanda and Mount Hurrum," Lugalbanda makes long journeys across mountains.

pp. 103–4, *The elders turned to Enkidu and said, / "We leave the king in your care. Protect him, / guide him through all the treacherous passes, / show him where to find food and where / to dig for fresh water, lead him to the Forest / and fight at his side:* Literally, "In this our assembly [we leave the king in your care]. Make sure that he returns and bring [the king back into our care]."

p. 104, *May Shamash help you, / may the gods grant you your heart's desire:* From OB III, ll. 285–86.

p. 104, *Enkidu said to Gilgamesh* through *to the Cedar Forest, where Humbaba lives":* From OB III, ll. 272 ff.

Book IV

p. 105, *At four hundred miles they stopped to eat, / at a thousand miles they pitched their camp. / They had traveled for just three days and nights:* Literally, "At 20 *bēr* (=216 kilometers, or about 134 miles) they stopped to eat, at 30 *bēr* (=324 km., 201 mi.) they pitched their camp, they had traveled 50 *bēr* (=540 km., 335 mi.) in a single day." There is some confusion in the text, which has the heroes pitching camp after one day, yet describes the actual camping and dream ritual as taking place every third evening, after a three-day march. For clarity's sake, I have inserted the three-day rather than the one-day distances.

p. 105, *Enkidu did the ritual for dreams:* Here I have followed the interpretation of Bottéro. "The ritual is one of incubation: of a dream 'obtained,' that is, asked of the gods and received in a place determined and protected from evil influences that could disturb or corrupt the process.

Here, it is the top of the mountain, which is a sacred place, nearer to heaven, the dwelling of Šamaš, who will certainly send the dream. Hence the use of *mašatu*, scented flour or powder, which was burned in fumigating offerings, the mantic ritual performed by Enkidu for Gilgameš (we know nothing about it), and the enchanted circle in which he encloses him at the moment when he is going to sleep and receive the desired dream. These circles were standard practice in rituals of magic and exorcism: drawn with flour, leaves, or branches, even with improvised barriers of reeds, in order to isolate the dreamer from all pernicious fluids. The gust of wind passing by is the sign that heaven has given its consent that the dream should take place, in the ordinary conditions, and thus with divinatory value, which of course the dreamer hopes will be favorable" (Bottéro, p. 99).

p. 106, *We were walking in a gorge, / and when I looked up, a huge mountain loomed, / so huge that we were as small as flies. / Then the mountain fell down on top of us. / Dear friend, tell me, what does this mean?*: Literally, "[in] a mountain valley, [the mountain] fell on [. . .], we, like [flies]."

p. 107, *Gilgamesh, happy with his good dream, / smiled, and his face lit up with pleasure*: From OB Schøyen₂, ll. 23–24. The second line also occurs in OB II, l. 104, in the description of Enkidu drunk; both lines occur in one of the Middle Babylonian Boğazköy fragments, MB Boğ₂, obverse, ll. 3′–4′.

p. 108, *I looked up and a huge mountain loomed, / it threw me down, it pinned me by the feet*: From MB Boğ₂, obverse, ll. 13′–14′.

p. 108, *a terrifying brightness hurt my eyes, / suddenly a young man appeared, / he was shining and handsome, he took me by the arm / he pulled me out from under the mountain:* From OB Schøyen₂, ll. 8 ff.

p. 108, *he gave me water, my heart grew calm.:* From MB Boğ₂, obverse, l. 18′.

p. 109, *Again, the mountain stands for Humbaba. / He threw you down, but he could not kill you:* From OB Schøyen₂, ll. 14 ff. Literally (in George's translation), "Now, my friend, the one to whom we go, / is he not the mountain? He is something very strange! / Now, Ḫuwawa to whom we go, / is he not the mountain? He is something very strange!"

p. 109, *As for the handsome young man who appeared, / he stands for Lord Shamash, who will rescue you / and grant you everything you desire:* From OB Schøyen₂, ll. 21–22.

p. 111, *The fiery heavens stand for Humbaba, / who tried to kill you with lightning and flames. / But in spite of the fire, he could not harm you. / We will kill Humbaba. Success is ours. / However he attacks us, we will prevail:* Literally (in Foster's translation), "Humbaba, like a god [. . .] / [. . .] the light flaring [. . .] / We will be [victorious] over him. / Humbaba aroused our fury [. . .] / [. . .] we will prevail over him. / Further, at dawn the word of Shamash will be in our favor."

pp. 112–13, *I have had a fourth dream* through *who came to your rescue was our lord, Shamash:* From the Old Babylonian excerpt tablet from Nippur, OB Nippur, ll. 9 ff.

pp. 112–13, *it grimaced at me, terrifying flames / shot from its mouth, then beside me I saw / a young man with an unearthly glow, / he seized the creature, he broke its wings, / he wrung its neck and threw it to the ground . . . The eagle that you saw, with a lion's head, / stands for Humbaba. Though it dived straight toward you / and terrifying flames shot from its mouth, / nothing could cause you harm. The young man / who came to your rescue was our lord, Shamash. / He will stand beside us when the monster attacks. / Whatever happens, we will prevail:* Literally, " 'It was [. . .], its face was strange, its jaws were fire, its breath was death. There was a strange-looking man [. . .] he was standing by me in my dream. [He . . .] its wings, he seized its arms, [. . .] then he threw it down [in front of] me. [. . .]' *[gap]* '[. . .] it [descended upon us, like a] cloud, it was [. . .], its face was strange, its jaws were fire, its breath was death. Though you were afraid of its terrifying aura, I will [. . .] its foot, I will enable you to get up. The man you saw was mighty Shamash."

pp. 115–16, *I was wrestling with a gigantic bull* through *we will achieve a triumph / greater than any man has achieved:* From one of the Old Babylonian Šaduppûm tablets, OB Harmal$_1$, ll. 4 ff.

p. 116, *They could hear Humbaba's terrifying roar:* From OB Schøyen$_2$, l. 57, where the line occurs after Gilgamesh's second dream.

pp. 116–17, *Gilgamesh stopped. He was trembling. Tears / flowed down his cheeks. "O Shamash," he cried, / "protect me on this dangerous journey. / Remember me, help me, hear my prayer." / They stood and listened. A moment passed. / Then, from heaven, the voice of the god / called to Gilgamesh: "Hurry, attack, / attack Humbaba while the time is right, / before he enters the depths of the forest, / before he can hide there and wrap himself / in his seven auras with their paralyzing glare. / He is wearing just one now. Attack him! Now!":* Literally, "[. . .] going [. . .] Uruk's midst, [. . .] stand there and [. . .] O Gilgamesh, scion sprung from Uruk [. . .]. [Shamash] heard what [he] had said, immediately a voice [called from the sky], 'Hurry, attack him, don't let him [escape into the forest], [don't let him] go down into the thicket or [. . .]. He hasn't yet wrapped himself in his seven terrifying auras [. . .], he is wrapped in only one, the six others are off."

p. 117, *He is wearing just one now. Attack him! Now!:* I have moved the rest of Tablet IV to Book V, except for two fragmentary passages, which I have omitted, and the last two lines, which remain as the conclusion of Book IV.

BOOK V

p. 118, *Gripping their axes, their knives unsheathed, / they entered the Forest and made their way through:* These lines actually occur slightly further on in Tablet V. Literally (in Foster's translation), "Axes touched with [the whetstone], / Daggers and swords [. . .] / One by one [. . .] / They crept forward [. . .] / Humbaba [. . .]."

p. 118, *the tangle of thorn bushes underfoot:* This line is followed by a fragmentary passage, which I have omitted.

pp. 118–22, *Suddenly Enkidu was seized by terror* through *Dear friend, great warrior, noble hero, / don't lose courage:* The text of the Standard Version is so fragmentary here and so full of gaps that I have borrowed at length from the Sumerian poem "Gilgamesh and Huwawa" (Version A). I have also added a few passages, as specified in the following notes. The Standard Version of this entire section reads literally, "Gilgamesh [. . .] Why

[. . .] [*gap*] Enlil [. . .] Enkidu [. . .] his mouth [. . .] of Humbaba [. . .] one by one [. . .] garments [. . .] On the treacherous path [. . .] two [. . .] Two triplets [. . .] A three-ply rope [. . .], two cubs are [. . .] than a strong lion. [*gap*]."

p. 118, *Suddenly Enkidu was seized by terror, / his face turned pale like a severed head:* From OB Schøyen₂, ll. 63 ff., following George's restoration.

pp. 118–19, *He said to Gilgamesh, "Dear friend, I cannot / continue, I am frightened, I cannot go on. / You go into the dreadful forest, / you kill Humbaba and win the fame. / I will return now to great-walled Uruk, / and all men will know what a coward I have been.":* This passage is an expansion of a single line (104) from "Gilgamesh and Huwawa": "Gilgamesh, you go further up into the mountains, but I will go back to the city."

p. 119, *Gilgamesh answered, "Dear friend, dear brother, / I cannot kill Humbaba alone. / Please stay here with me. Stand at my side:* I have added these lines.

p. 119, *'Two boats lashed together will never sink. / A three-ply rope is not easily broken.' / If we help each other and fight side by side, / what harm can come to us? Let us go on / and attack the monster. We have come so far. / Whatever you are feeling, let us go on:* From "Gilgamesh and Huwawa," ll. 107 ff. Literally, "Enkidu, two people together will not die. A man tied to his boat will not drown. No one can tear apart a three-ply cloth. Water can't wash someone away from a city wall. Fire in a reed house can't be extinguished. If you help me and I help you, what can anyone do against us? When a boat sinks, when a boat sinks, when a boat headed for Magan sinks, when the *magilum* barge

sinks, the boat that is lashed tight to another boat holds steady. Come
now, let us go to him and see him face to face."

p. 119, *Two boats lashed together will never sink. / A three-ply rope is not easily broken*:
These two expressions are proverbial. The second was still proverbial
more than fifteen hundred years after "Gilgamesh and Huwawa," as we
can see from Ecclesiastes 4:9–12: "Two are better than one, because they
have a good reward for their labor. For if one of them falls, the other will
lift him up; but how unfortunate is he who is alone when he falls and
doesn't have another to lift him up. Again, if two lie together, they are
warm; but how can one be warm alone? And though someone might
prevail against a man who is alone, two can withstand him. A three-ply
rope is not quickly broken."

pp. 119–20, *Enkidu said, "You have never met him, / so you don't know the horror that
lurks ahead. / But when I saw him, my blood ran cold. / His teeth are knife-sharp, they
stick out like tusks, / his face, blood-smeared, is a lion's face, / he charges ahead like a rag-
ing torrent, / his forehead ablaze. Who can withstand him? / I am terrified. I cannot go
on."*: From "Gilgamesh and Huwawa," ll. 98 ff. Literally, "Since you
haven't seen him, he doesn't frighten you. But I have seen him and he
terrified me. His teeth are dragon's teeth, his face is a lion's face, his
chest is a raging torrent, his forehead is a fire that devours the reed
thickets and no one can escape it."

pp. 120–21, *Gilgamesh said, "Courage, dear brother* through *we will stamp our fame
on men's minds forever."*: I have transferred this passage here from the end of
Tablet IV.

p. 121, *They walked deep into the Cedar Forest, / gripping their axes, their knives unsheathed, / following the trail that Humbaba had made:* I have added these lines.

p. 121, *They came within sight of the monster's den. / He was waiting inside it. Their blood ran cold. / He saw the two friends, he grimaced, he bared / his teeth, he let out a deafening roar. / He glared at Gilgamesh. "Young man," he said, / "you will never go home. Prepare to die." / Dread surged through Gilgamesh, terror flooded / his muscles, his heart froze, his mouth went dry, / his legs shook, his feet were rooted to the ground:* From "Gilgamesh and Huwawa," ll. 122 ff. Literally, "Huwawa sat in his house among the cedars. He glared at Gilgamesh and Enkidu, it was the look of death. He shook his head at them, it was the sign of doom. When he spoke, his words were few: 'You, young man, will never return to the city where your mother gave birth to you.' Fear and terror spread through Gilgamesh's muscles and limbs, his feet were rooted to the ground."

pp. 121–22, *"Dear friend, great warrior, noble hero, / don't lose courage:* From "Gilgamesh and Huwawa," ll. 130 ff. Literally, "Powerful champion, noble hero, delight of the gods, strong bull charging to battle, your mother knew well how to bear a son, your wet nurse knew well how to nourish a child at her breast. Do not be afraid, rest your hands on the ground."

p. 122, *remember this: / 'Two boats lashed together will never sink. / A three-ply rope is not easily broken.' / If we help each other and fight side by side, / what harm can come to us? Let us go on:* I have repeated this from an earlier passage.

p. 122, *They advanced to the monster's den. Humbaba / charged out roaring at them and said:* I have added these lines.

p. 122, *I will tear you limb from limb, I will crush you / and leave you bloody and mangled on the ground:* I have added these lines.

p. 123, *you both stand before me looking like a pair / of frightened girls:* Literally, "You stand here a hostile stranger."

p. 123, *How dreadful Humbaba's face has become! / It is changing into a thousand nightmare / faces, more horrible than I can bear. / I feel haunted. I am too afraid to go on:* Literally, "My friend, Humbaba's face has changed. We marched like heroes toward his [den] to defeat him, but the heart that grew frightened doesn't grow calm in a moment."

pp. 123–24, *We must not hesitate or retreat. / Two intimate friends cannot be defeated. / Be courageous. Remember how strong you are. / I will stand by you. Now let us attack:* Literally (in George's translation), "Now, my friend, there is a single . . . / To gather up the copper (ingots) from the channel moulds of the copper-founder? / To blow on the coals for a double hour, to . . . what is alight for a double hour? / To send the Deluge is to crack the whip! / [Do not] pull back your foot, do not make a retreat! [. . .] . . . make your blow good and strong!"

p. 124, *Gilgamesh felt his courage return:* I have added this line.

p. 124, *They charged at Humbaba like two wild bulls* through *his roar boomed forth like a blast of thunder:* I have transferred this passage here from the end of Tablet IV.

p. 124, *split the mountains of Lebanon:* "Lebanon and Hermon are separated by a deep crevasse (the Rift Valley) which continues to the Gulf of Aqaba and beyond. By a new imaginary etiology, the authors of this passage seem to have put in terms of cause and effect the struggle of the giants and this geological state of things" (Bottéro, p. 115).

p. 124, *a sulfurous fog / descended on them and made their eyes ache:* Literally, "death rained down on them like a mist."

p. 125, *Humbaba said, "Gilgamesh, have mercy. / Let me live here in the Cedar Forest. / If you spare my life, I will be your slave, / I will give you as many cedars as you wish. / You are king of Uruk by the grace of Shamash, / honor him with a cedar temple / and a glorious cedar palace for yourself. / All this is yours, if only you spare me.":* Literally, "Begging for his life, Humbaba said to Gilgamesh, 'You are so young, Gilgamesh, your mother gave birth to you and indeed you are the son of [Ninsun, the Lady of the Wild Cows]. [. . .] the command of Shamash, lord of the mountain: "Gilgamesh, the heir of Uruk, will be king." [. . .] Gilgamesh, a dead man can't [. . .], a living [. . .] his master. Spare my life, Gilgamesh [. . .] Let me dwell here for you in [. . .] as many trees as you wish [. . .], I will guard the myrtle for you, the [. . .], timber, the pride of a palace.' "

pp. 125–26, *"If any mortal, / Enkidu, knows the rules of my forest, / it is you. You know that this is my place / and that I am the forest's guardian. Enlil / put me here to terrify men, / and I guard the forest as Enlil ordains. / If you kill me, you will call down the gods' / wrath, and their judgment will be severe:* Literally, "You know the rules of my forest, the rules of [. . .], so you understand what has been ordained."

p. 126, *Shamash in Larsa:* There is an alternate reading: "Shamash in Sippar."

p. 126, *who killed Humbaba in the Cedar Forest:* Here I have omitted two brief fragmentary passages and a repetition of the passage that begins "Enkidu said, 'Dear friend, quickly' " and ends with " 'who killed Humbaba in the Cedar Forest.' "

pp. 127–28, *Knowing he was doomed, Humbaba cried out, / "I curse you both. Because you have done this, / may Enkidu die, may he die in great pain, / may Gilgamesh be inconsolable, / may his merciless heart be crushed with grief." // Gilgamesh dropped his axe, appalled. / Enkidu said, "Courage, dear friend. / Close your ears to Humbaba's curses. / Don't listen to a word. Slaughter him! Now!" // Gilgamesh, hearing his beloved friend, / came to himself. He yelled, he lifted / his massive axe, he swung it, it tore / into Humbaba's neck, the blood / shot out, again the axe bit flesh / and bone, the monster staggered, his eyes / rolled, and at the axe's third stroke / he toppled like a cedar and crashed to the ground. / At his death-roar the mountains of Lebanon shook, / the valleys ran with his blood, for ten miles / the forest resounded. Then the two friends / sliced him open, pulled out his intestines, / cut off his head with its knife-sharp teeth / and horrible bloodshot staring eyes. / A gentle rain fell onto the mountains. / A gentle rain fell onto the mountains:* Literally " 'May they never [. . .] May the two of them not grow old, and, like his friend Gilgamesh, may Enkidu have no one to bury him.' Enkidu opened his mouth and said to Gilgamesh, 'My friend, I speak to you, but you don't listen to me. Until the curse [. . .] to his mouth.' [. . .] of his friend, he drew the knife at his side, Gilgamesh [struck him] in the neck, Enkidu [. . .] until he pulled out the lungs. [. . .] jumping up, [from] the head he took the tusks as a prize. [. . .] in abundance fell on the mountain, [. . .] in abundance fell on the mountain." To the Standard Version of this passage I have added a passage from the Old Babylonian excerpt tablet from

Nērebtum, OB Ishchali, reverse, ll. 25′ ff.: "the valleys ran with his blood, he struck Huwawa the guardian to the ground, for two leagues [. . .] in the distance. With him he struck [. . .], the forests [. . .], he killed the monster, the forest's guardian, at whose shout Sirion and Lebanon were split apart, [. . .] the mountains [. . .] all the highlands trembled."

p. 128, *A gentle rain fell onto the mountains:* "Rain" is a conjecture of Tournay and Shaffer.

p. 128, *They took their axes and penetrated / deeper into the forest:* From OB Ishchali, reverse, l. 37′.

p. 128, *they went / chopping down cedars, the woods chips flew, / Gilgamesh chopped down the mighty trees, / Enkidu hewed the trunks into timbers:* Literally, "[. . .] one-fifth of a cubit was the [. . .] of their (cedar) shavings. Gilgamesh cut down the trees, Enkidu chose the best timber."

pp. 128–29, *Enkidu said, "By your great strength* through *may it be a joy to the people of Nippur.":* From the Old Babylonian tablet at the Iraq Museum in Baghdad, OB IM, ll. 19 ff.

BOOK VI

p. 130, *he took off his filthy, blood-spattered clothes, / put on a tunic of the finest wool, / wrapped himself in a glorious gold-trimmed / purple robe and fastened it with / a wide fringed belt, then put on his crown:* Literally, "He took off his filthy clothes, he put on clean ones, he wrapped himself in a royal robe, tied on a wide belt. Gilgamesh put on his crown." "The purple candys embroidered with gold was reserved for the king" (Wilcox, *The Mode in Costume*).

p. 130, *The goddess Ishtar caught sight of him, / she saw how splendid a man he was, / her heart was smitten, her loins caught fire*: Literally, "The princess Ishtar looked with desire on Gilgamesh's beauty."

p. 130, *marry me*: "Probably as a ruse, and to attract him to her bed, since she has never been either a wife or a mother in the proper sense of the word, Ishtar proposes a real marriage. Thus, before referring to all the claims of gifts that she will demand, he will later ironically bring up the question of the compensatory payment (called *terḫatu*) that the future husband or his family has to make to the family of the future wife" (Bottéro, p. 123).

p. 131, *I will give you abundance beyond your dreams: / marble and alabaster, ivory and jade*: I have added these lines.

p. 131, *servants with blue-green eyes*: I have followed Tournay and Shaffer in adding this phrase from MB Boǧ₂, reverse, l. 7.

p. 131, *guide-horns of amber*: "The 'horns' of a chariot are probably the yoke terminals, which are made of alabaster on Egyptian New Kingdom chariots, and in Middle Bronze Age tablets from Mari. *elmēšu*-stone: a lustrous, precious, semi-mythical stone, possibly amber, often used with rock crystal" (Dalley, p. 129).

p. 131, *storm-demons:* "The *ūmu* . . . is the lion-headed monster that pulls the chariots of the storm god Adad, the sun, the warriors Ninurta and Marduk and the warlike Ištar" (George, *BGE,* II, p. 830).

p. 131, *And I will bless everything that you own . . . These are the least of the gifts I will shower / upon you. Come here. Be my sweet man:* I have added these lines.

p. 132, *Gilgamesh said, "Your price is too high, / such riches are far beyond my means. / Tell me, how could I ever repay you, / even if I give you jewels, perfumes, / rich robes? And what will happen to me / when your heart turns elsewhere and your lust burns out?:* Literally (in Foster's translation), "[What shall I give you] if I take you to wife? / [Shall I give you] a headdress (?) for your person, or clothing? / [Shall I give you] bread or drink? / [Shall I give you] food worthy of divinity? / [Shall I give you] drink, worthy of queenship? / Shall I bind [. . .]? / Shall I heap up [. . .]? / [. . .] for a garment?"

p. 132, *a mouse that gnaws through its thin reed shelter:* Following Tournay and Shaffer.

p. 132, *limestone that crumbles and undermines / a solid stone wall:* "The image is of a friable element built into a wall made of heavier stones" (Bottéro, p. 125).

p. 132, *a battering ram / that knocks down the rampart of an allied city:* I have followed Bottéro's interpretation here.

p. 133, *Which could satisfy your endless desires?:* Literally (following Speiser), "Which of your lovers pleased you for all time?"

p. 133, *Let me remind you of how they suffered, / how each one came to a bitter end:* Literally, "Come, let me count your lovers."

p. 133, *sent him to the underworld:* In the Sumerian poem "The Descent of Inanna," after Inanna's (=Ishtar's) ascent from hell, demons demand a substitute for her; she gives them Dumuzi (=Tammuz), and they carry him down to hell in her place.

p. 133, *the bright-speckled roller bird:* "We know nothing about the love affair of Ishtar with the 'roller bird,' or of her love affairs with the two animals that follow" (Bottéro, p. 125).

p. 133, *Ow-ee! Ow-ee!:* "In Akkadian, the cry of the bird is . . . *kappî* ('My wings!'), which evokes a sort of plaintive whining. The story is etiological" (Bottéro, p. 126).

p. 133, *you dug seven pits for him, / and when he fell, you left him to die:* Literally, "You dug seven and seven pits for him."

p. 133, *endlessly:* Literally, "7 double leagues" = about 45 miles; in other words, a great distance.

p. 133, *to muddy his own water:* "Horses put their front feet in the water when drinking, churning up mud" (Kovacs, p. 52).

p. 134, *the goddess Silili:* The myth is unknown, as are the myths of the shepherd and of Ishullanu.

p. 134, *'Sweet Ishullanu, let me suck your rod, / touch my vagina, caress my jewel'*: Literally, "O my Ishullanu, let me eat your vigor, reach out your hand [*or* penis] and touch my vulva."

pp. 134–35, *But you kept up your sweet-talk and at last he gave in, / then you changed, you turned him into*: Literally, "When he had finished speaking, you struck him, you turned him into . . ." I have changed the story here for the sake of consistency, since all the other examples are of men who became Ishtar's lovers and suffered as a result.

p. 135, *toad*: I have followed Bottéro here. Other scholars have translated this hapax legomenon as "dwarf," "mole," "spider," or "scarecrow."

p. 135, *her father, Anu*: In other Mesopotamian traditions, Ishtar is the daughter of Sîn and granddaughter of Anu, and/or she is Anu's consort.

p. 136, *ghouls will ascend to devour the living, / and the living will be outnumbered by the dead*: "These two verses are found also in the Akkadian myth of 'The Descent of Ishtar to the Underworld' and in 'Nergal and Ereshkigal,' and there is no way of knowing which of the three is the model or source" (Bottéro, p. 129).

p. 136, *Uruk will have famine for seven long years. / Have you provided the people with grain / for seven years, and the cattle with fodder?*: Literally, "for seven years let the widow of Uruk gather chaff, [and the farmer of Uruk] grow hay."

p. 137, *ten feet*: Literally, "7 cubits."

p. 137, *Gilgamesh rushed in and shouted, "Dear friend, / keep fighting, together we are sure to win."*: I have added these lines and omitted the following passage: "Enkidu opened his mouth [to speak] and said to Gilgamesh, 'My friend, we boasted [. . .] city, how should we answer the crowds of people? My friend, I have observed the strength of the Bull of Heaven, so knowing its strength [I know] that our strength is sufficient. I will [circle] behind it, I will seize [it by its tail], I will set [my foot on its haunch], in [. . .]. Then [you,] like a [brave,] skilled [butcher,] thrust your dagger between its shoulders and the base of its horns.' "

p. 139, *her priestesses, / those who offer themselves to all men / in her honor*: Literally, "her *kezertu-, ḫarīmtu-,* and *šamḫātu*-women": three classes of cultic prostitute-priestesses.

p. 139, *thirty pounds*: 30 *mina* = 15 kg.= 33 lbs.

p. 139, *four hundred gallons*: 6 *kor* = 1,500 l. = 396 gal.

p. 139, *in the chapel / dedicated to Lugalbanda*: Literally, "in the room of the head of the family." "Rather than a bedroom in the palace of Uruk, this was probably a chapel in the temple, consecrated to Lugalbanda. The votive horns, filled with ointments with a base of fragrant oil, were supposed to serve in some ceremonial rite of dressing and anointing the image of Gilgameš's deified father" (Bottéro, p. 133).

p. 140, *The two friends washed themselves in the river*: "In ancient times the Euphrates flowed through Uruk. It is possible that the washing had a religious sense and that the two heroes intended to purify themselves of the defilement contracted by the killing of the supernatural Bull" (Bot-téro, p. 133).

p. 140, *singing girls:* Following Speiser.

p. 140, *Enkidu—he is . . . :* Following Bottéro.

BOOK VII

pp. 141–42, *"Beloved brother,"* Enkidu said through *and never will I see my dear brother again."*: From the Hittite version, Tablet III, § 1, ll. 2 ff. The Standard Version begins with Enkidu's long, rather silly speech to the door, which I have omitted.

p. 141, *Then Enlil said to him, 'Enkidu, / not Gilgamesh, is the one who must die.'*: I have omitted the following lines from the Hittite version: "Then the sun god of heaven said to heroic Enlil, 'Wasn't it at my command that they killed the Bull of Heaven and also Humbaba? Enkidu is innocent—should he then die?' Enlil grew angry at the sun god of heaven and said, 'You are speaking like that because you accompanied them every day like a friend.' " "The Standard Version seems to originate from a different tradition, in which Šamaš as well is squarely opposed to the killing of Humbaba" (Bottéro, p. 287). See p. 126, "before the great gods can get enraged, / Enlil in Nippur, Shamash in Larsa."

p. 142, *Enkidu said, "Beloved brother, / last night I had a second bad dream:* This passage occurs later in Tablet VII; I have inserted it here and divided Gilgamesh's response to the first dream into two speeches.

p. 144, *Etana . . . Sumuqan . . . Ereshkigal . . . Belet-seri:* See glossary.

p. 144, *so it is a healthy man who has dreamed this:* "In order to reassure his friend, Gilgameš sees (or pretends to see) the dream as an excellent omen, interpreting it by the principle of 'inversion' . . . Further on in this passage, it is obvious that in fact Gilgameš had no doubt about the fatal character of the dream" (Bottéro, p. 138).

p. 145, *and to Ea the wise:* Literally (according to George's restoration), "*may* [*my entreaty. . . . . . . .to Ea*]." "It is difficult to avoid the conclusion that these three lines report Gilgameš's intentions to solicit the aid not of Enlil alone but of the great divine triad, Anu, Enlil and Ea" (George, *BGE,* II, p. 846).

p. 145, *a gold statue made in your image:* "The image of a person . . . placed in the sanctuary was . . . , by its very presence, supposed to perpetually 'pray' on behalf of that person to the god it was dedicated to" (Bottéro, p. 138).

p. 145, *Don't worry, dear friend, you will soon get better, / this votive image will restore you to health:* I have added these lines following Bottéro's interpretation.

p. 145, *"I turn to you, Lord, / since suddenly fate has turned against me:* Literally, "I appeal to you, Shamash, on account of my precious life."

pp. 145–146, *As for that wretched trapper who found me / when I was free in the wilderness— / because he destroyed my life, destroy / his livelihood, may he go home empty, / may no animals ever enter his traps, / or if they do, may they vanish like mist, / and may he starve for bringing me here:* Literally (in Foster's translation), "As for that hunter, the entrapping-man, / Who did not let me get as much life as my friend, / May that hunter not get enough to make him a living. / Make his profit loss, cut down his take, / May his income, his portion evaporate before you, / Any wildlife that enters [his traps], make it go out the window!"

p. 146, *may your man prefer younger, prettier girls:* Following Foster's conjecture.

p. 146, *may he beat you as a housewife beats a rug:* Literally, "[. . .] of the potter." I have gone in the same direction (though with a different image) as Foster's conjecture "[may he pinch you] like potter's clay."

pp. 146–47, *may your roof keep leaking and no carpenter fix it* through *and the rabble mock you as you walk the streets:* I have changed the order of the images here.

p. 146, *may wild dogs camp in your bedroom:* From the Middle Babylonian Ur tablet, MB Ur, l. 32.

p. 147, *a bed of honor:* "The 'bed' is the catafalque where the corpse is laid out before the funeral. The next lines recall the place of honor that the king of Uruk had given him during his lifetime. We don't know why the seat of repose is 'on his left' " (Bottéro, p. 142).

p. 149, *Then Enkidu said to Gilgamesh:* I have added this line. There are several gaps and fragments that precede Enkidu's speech, and it is followed by another fragmentary line: "Gilgamesh said, 'My friend saw a dream that [will] not . . . ' "

p. 149, *For twelve long days / he was deathly sick, he lay in his bed / in agony, unable to rest, / and every day he grew worse:* Literally, "One day, a second day, Enkidu was sick, he lay in his bed. A third and a fourth day Enkidu [. . .]. A fifth, a sixth and a seventh, an eighth, a ninth [and tenth day] Enkidu was sick [. . .], an eleventh and a twelfth day [. . .] Enkidu [. . .] in his bed."

p. 149, *"Have you abandoned me now, dear friend? / You told me that you would come to help me / when I was afraid. But I cannot see you, / you have not come to fight off this danger. / Yet weren't we to remain forever / inseparable, you and I?":* In this speech I have followed the interpretation of Bottéro. Literally (in George's translation): "[My god] has spurned me, my friend, [. . . ,] / like one who in the midst of battle [. . .] / I was afraid of combat [. . . ,] / my friend, he who in combat [. . .] / I, in [*combat, . . .*]."

p. 150, *When he heard the death rattle, Gilgamesh moaned / like a dove. His face grew dark. "Beloved, / wait, don't leave me. Dearest of men, / don't die, don't let them take you from me":* From the Middle Babylonian Megiddo tablet, MB Megiddo, reverse, ll. 14′ ff. Literally (in Kovacs's translation): "At his noises Gilgamesh was roused [. . .] / Like a dove he moaned [. . .] / 'May he not be held, in death [. . .] / O preeminent among men [. . .] / To his friend [. . .] / 'I will mourn him (?) / I at his side [. . .]' "

BOOK VIII

p. 152, *Ulaya:* Literally, "May the holy River Ulaya mourn you, along whose banks we once proudly walked." This line seems to refer to an episode that has not survived in the extant tablets.

pp. 152–53, *my beloved friend is dead, he is dead, / my beloved brother is dead, I will mourn / as long as I breathe, I will sob for him / like a woman who has lost her only child:* Literally, "I will mourn Enkidu, my friend, I will sob for him like a hired mourning woman." (Professional mourners were valued for their loud and passionate laments.)

p. 153, *swift stallion, wild deer:* Literally, "swift mule, quick wild ass of the mountains."

pp. 154–55, *Let obsidian and all other beautiful stones— / a thousand jewels of every color— / be piled along with the silver and gold / and sent on a barge, down the Euphrates / to great-walled Uruk, for Enkidu's statue:* Added from the apocryphal "Letter of Gilgamesh" (seventh century BCE?), which helps to flesh out the description of the statue. I have also made the next lines in the Standard Version ("I will lay him down . . . in a lion skin") part of the proclamation, changing the second-person to third-person pronouns.

p. 155, *surveyed his riches:* I have omitted a fragmentary passage here.

p. 156, *He closed his eyes, in his mind he formed* through *he spread out each one in front of Shamash:* I have moved this passage forward from the end of Tablet VIII.

p. 156, *precious yew wood:* "The precious wood called *elammaku*, not identified, came from the northwest (Syria) and was used primarily for furniture" (Bottéro, p. 154).

p. 156, *a carnelian bowl . . . a lapis lazuli bowl:* "Red was the color of mourning . . . Red and blue are found together more than once in the ancient

Mesopotamian texts, particularly in the context of the hereafter and of mourning" (Bottéro, p. 154).

p. 156, *a polished javelin of pure cedar:* Literally, "[a *throw*]stick of . . . , the pure wood."

p. 156, *"Let Ishtar accept this:* This respectful passage, along with VII 160 ("May Ishtar, [the ablest] of the gods, introduce you to a man"), is another indication that Book VI was added to the main body of the poem, perhaps by Sîn-lēqi-unninni.

p. 157, *a golden necklace . . . a mirror:* Schrott's conjectures.

p. 158, *When all the offerings were set out:* There is one additional offering, of an alabaster flask to "[Dumuzi]-abzu, blame-bearer of the underworld," which I have omitted, along with a short, fragmentary passage.

p. 158, *After the funeral, Gilgamesh went out / from Uruk, into the wilderness / with matted hair, in a lion skin:* There is a gap at the end of Tablet VIII. I have added these lines.

BOOK IX

p. 159, *How can I bear this sorrow / that gnaws at my belly, this fear of death / that restlessly drives me onward? If only / I could find the one man whom the gods made immortal, / I would ask him how to overcome death:* Literally, "Sorrow has entered my heart. I have become afraid of death, so I roam the wilderness. I am on the road and will travel quickly to Utnapishtim, son of Ubartutu." I have

omitted the following passage: " 'When I arrived at night at mountain passes, I saw some lions and was afraid, I looked up and prayed to the moon, to [. . .] lamp of the gods: "O [Sîn and . . . ,] keep me safe."' [Gilgamesh] arose, he woke up from the dream. [. . .] presence of the moon he rejoiced to be alive. He lifted the axe, he drew [the dagger from] his belt, he fell on them like an arrow, he struck the [lions, he] killed and scattered them." The rest of the passage is fragmentary.

p. 159, *So Gilgamesh roamed, his heart full of anguish,* / *wandering, always eastward, in search* / *of Utnapishtim, whom the gods made immortal:* I have added these lines.

p. 161, *"Gilgamesh is my name," he answered,* / *"I am the king of great-walled Uruk* / *and have come here to find my ancestor* / *Utnapishtim, who joined the assembly* / *of the gods, and was granted eternal life.* / *He is my last hope. I want to ask him* / *how he managed to overcome death.":* Literally, "[. . .] the [. . .] of my ancestor, Utnapishtim, who joined the assembly of the gods and [. . .], of death and life [. . .]."

pp. 161–63, *"No one is able* / *to cross the Twin Peaks, nor has anyone ever* / *entered the tunnel into which the sun* / *plunges when it sets and moves through the earth.* / *Inside the tunnel there is total darkness:* / *deep is the darkness, with no light at all."* // *The scorpion woman said, "This brave man,* / *driven by despair, his body frost-chilled,* / *exhausted, and burnt by the desert sun—* / *show him the way to Utnapishtim."* // *The scorpion man said, "Ever downward* / *through the deep darkness the tunnel leads.* / *All will be pitch black before and behind you,* / *all will be pitch black to either side.* / *You must run through the tunnel faster than the wind.* / *You have just twelve hours. If you don't emerge* / *from the tunnel before the sun sets and enters,* / *you will find no refuge from its deadly fire.* / *Penetrate into the mountains' depths,* / *may the Twin Peaks lead you safely to your goal,* / *may they safely take you to the edge of the world.* / *The gate to the tunnel lies here before*

you. / Go now in peace, and return in peace.": Literally, " 'Never, Gilgamesh, has anyone [. . .], never has anyone [. . .] the mountain. Its interior [. . .] for twelve double hours (*or* twelve double leagues = 80 miles), the darkness is dense, there is no [light]. At the rising of the sun [. . .], at the setting of the [. . .]. At the setting of the [. . .] they sent forth [. . .] And you, how [. . .] Will you go [. . .]?' [*long gap*] 'Through sorrow [. . .], by cold and sunshine [. . .], through exhaustion [. . .]. Now you [. . .].' The scorpion-man [opened his mouth and said] to Gilgamesh [. . .], 'Go, Gilgamesh [. . .] May the Twin Peaks [. . .] The mountain ranges [. . .] In safety may [. . .].' "

p. 162, *This brave man:* Following Foster, I have assigned this speech to the scorpion woman.

p. 163, *For a second and a third hour Gilgamesh ran, / deep was the darkness, with no light at all / before and behind him and to either side:* Literally, "For a second hour [he ran], deep was the darkness, [with no light at all], he could see [nothing in front and behind him]. For a third hour [he ran], [deep was the darkness, with no light at all, he could see nothing in front and behind him]." The same phrases are repeated for each of the twelve hours.

BOOK X

p. 165, *her golden pot-stand and brewing vat:* Literally, "She had pot-stands, she had [. . .]." "It is conventional to restore the end of this line after the Hittite version, which states that Šiduri had . . . 'a vat of gold' " (George, *BGE*, II, p. 868). "Some Mesopotamian drinking cups were conical, with

pointed bottoms, so they were set in a wooden rack to hold them up when they were full of liquid" (Foster, p. 72).

p. 166, *"Gilgamesh is my name," he said. / "I am the king of great-walled Uruk. / I am the man who killed Humbaba / in the Cedar Forest, I am the man / who triumphed over the Bull of Heaven." // Shiduri said, "Why are your cheeks so hollow:* Literally, "Gilgamesh spoke to her, to the tavern keeper: '[. . .] who killed the guardian, who seized the Bull of Heaven and killed the Bull of Heaven, who destroyed Humbaba in the Cedar Forest, who killed lions in the mountain passes.' The tavern keeper spoke to him, to Gilgamesh: '[If . . .] who killed the guardian, who seized the Bull of Heaven and killed the Bull of Heaven, who destroyed Humbaba in the Cedar Forest, who killed lions in the mountain passes, why are your cheeks hollow. . . .' "

p. 167, *thinking, 'If my grief is violent enough, / perhaps he will come back to life again.':* From the Old Babylonian tablet reportedly from Sippar, OB VA+BM, l. ii 7.

pp. 168–69, *Shiduri said, "Gilgamesh, where are you roaming?* through *when my heart is sick for Enkidu who died?:* From OB VA+BM, ll. iii 1 ff.

p. 168, *Humans are born, they live, then they die, / this is the order that the gods have decreed. / But until the end comes, enjoy your life, / spend it in happiness, not despair:* I have added these lines.

p. 168, *make each of your days / a delight:* A common theme in ancient Near Eastern wisdom literature. The most famous example is Ecclesiastes 9:7–10: "Go your way, eat your bread with joy, and drink your wine with

a merry heart, for God has already accepted what you do. At all times let your garments be white, and let there be oil on your head. Live joyfully with the wife you love, all the days of your insubstantial life that he has given you under the sun, all your insubstantial days, for that is your portion in life and in the work you work at under the sun. Whatever your hand finds to do, do it with all your might; for there is no work or thought or knowledge or wisdom in the grave to which you are going."

p. 170, *Stone Men:* I have followed the interpretation of Bottéro (the Akkadian word is often translated "Stone Things"). "This word remains a *crux* of *The Epic of Gilgameš.* It is not attested elsewhere. There is hardly any doubt that it refers to human beings or humanoids, since they accompany Urshanabi into the forest ... The famous myth called *Lugal-e* ... deals at length (but differently from here) with 'stone men' = men changed into stone [more accurately, stones turned into servants—S. M.] ... The *'Stone Ones'* are thus, in one way or another, like animated statues; that is also what the Hittite Version calls them ... We will see ... that they were indispensable for the crossing of the Waters of Death, undoubtedly because, being able, by their substance, to enter the deadly water with impunity, it was possible for them to push or pull the boat ... People have tried in various ways to rationalize these mysterious beings, by inferring, for example, that they are instruments or procedures of navigation: this is perhaps to forget that the story is pure myth!" (Bottéro, p. 170).

p. 170, *saw the axe flash, and he stood there, dazed.* / *Fear gripped the Stone Men who crewed the boat:* Literally, "he took his axe, he [...] him. But he, Gilgameš, hit his (Urshanabi's) head [...,] / he seized his arm and [...] his chest.

And the Stone Men [George: would seal] the boat, who did not fear the Waters of Death."

p. 171, *Gilgamesh came back and stood before him* through *through the underworld, where the sun comes forth:* From OB VA+BM, ll. iv 2 ff. I have omitted the Standard Version's continuation, which is a word-for-word repetition of the portion of Gilgamesh's dialogue with Shiduri that begins "Why are your cheeks so hollow" and ends "And won't I have to lie down in the dirt / like him, and never arise again?" It is repeated a third time in the dialogue with Utnapishtim.

pp. 171–72, *since in your fury / you have smashed the Stone Men, who crewed my boat / and could not be injured by the Waters of Death:* From OB VA+BM, ll. iv 24–25.

p. 172, *But don't despair. There is one more way / we can cross the vast ocean:* I have added these lines.

p. 172, *a hundred feet:* Literally, "5 *ninda*" (1 *ninda* = 12 cubits), or 90 feet. "This was the maximum depth of the ocean bottom [beneath the Waters of Death]. Since he is stronger and more vigorous, Gilgameš . . . will handle the poles when the time comes, plunging each one in turn into the Waters to propel the boat, up to the moment when it is almost entirely immersed and, in order not to have any contact with the water it is drenched in, he will have to drop it and take another. In other words, the Waters of Death were neither very deep nor very extensive" (Bottéro, p. 174).

p. 172, *grips*: "A point of metal resembling a nipple and meant to give the pole a firmer grip on the ocean bottom, without risk of slipping" (Bottéro, p. 174).

pp. 172–73, *Now be careful, / take up the first pole, push us forward, / and do not touch the Waters of Death. / When you come to the end of the first pole, drop it, / take up a second and a third one, until / you come to the end of the three-hundredth pole / and the Waters of Death are well behind us*: Literally, "[Stand back], Gilgamesh. Take [the first pole], don't let your hand be touched by the Waters of Death. Take a second, a third, and a fourth pole, Gilgamesh, take a fifth, a sixth, and a seventh pole, Gilgamesh, take an eighth, a ninth, and a tenth pole, Gilgamesh, take an eleventh and a twelfth pole, Gilgamesh."

pp. 173–74, *"Where are the Stone Men who crew the boat? / Why is there a stranger on board? / I have never seen him. Who can he be?" // Gilgamesh landed. When he saw the old man, / he said to him, "Tell me, where can I find / Utnapishtim, who joined the assembly / of the gods and was granted eternal life?"*: Literally, " 'Why have the boat's [. . .] been broken, and why is someone who is not its master aboard it? He who comes is no man of mine, and on the right [. . .]. I look, but he is no [man of] mine, I look, but he is no [. . .] I look, [. . .] me [. . .]. No [. . .] of mine [. . .]. The boatman [. . .] the man whom I [. . .], whom I watch is not [. . .] maybe the wilderness [. . .] the pine [. . .]' Gilgamesh approached the quay [. . .] he sent down [. . .] and he, he came up and he [. . .] Gilgamesh said to him, '[. . .] live Utnapishtim, son of Ubar[tutu]. [. . .] after the Flood which for [. . .] the Flood, what for [. . .].' "

p. 176, *let it be sealed shut with tar and pitch:* I have omitted two fragmentary lines that follow: "Because of me [*they*] *shall* not [. . .] the dancing, / because of me, happy and carefree, *they will* . . . [. . .]" (tr. George).

p. 177, *an old rope:* George's conjecture.

p. 177, *and a frantic, senseless, dissatisfied mind:* Literally (in George's translation): "Because he has no *advisors* [. . . ,] / (because) he has no words of counsel [. . . . . .]."

p. 177, *At night the moon travels across the sky* through *the world is established, from ancient times:* I have moved these lines to a bit later in Utnapishtim's speech and have omitted a fragmentary passage.

BOOK XI

p. 181, *when the great gods decided to send the Flood:* Two lines that occur later in Tablet XI imply that the Enlil's motivation was to punish men's evildoing: "do not allow all men / to die because of the sins of some" ("i.e., punish the guilty but not the innocent," George, *BGE* II, p. 891). In this it resembles the Noah stories, both in the J version:

> Now when the Lord saw how great the evil of humans was, and how every impulse in their hearts was nothing but evil all the time, he was sorry that he had made humans on the earth, and he was pained in his heart. And he said, "I will destroy all humankind from the earth: I am sorry I ever made them" (Genesis 6:5–7, from

Stephen Mitchell, *Genesis: A New Translation of the Classic Biblical Stories,* HarperCollins, 1996, p. 13).

and in the P version:

And the earth was exceedingly corrupt and filled with violence. And when God saw how corrupt the earth was and how corrupt humankind had become on the earth, God said to Noah, "I am going to put an end to humankind, for the earth is filled with violence because of them: I am going to blot them out from the earth" (Genesis 6:11–13; ibid., p. 15).

The *Atrahasis,* however, in its sublimely ridiculous way, provides the following motivation:

The earth was too full, the people too numerous,
the land was bellowing like a wild bull.
Enlil said to the other great gods,
"The noise of humans has become too loud,
their constant uproar is keeping me awake."

p. 181, *the Great Deep:* The vast, sweet-water, subterranean ocean (*apsû* in Akkadian) that was the domain of Ea; heaven and earth served as its roof.

p. 182, *They will all have all that they want, and more:* Literally, "a wealth of birds, a profusion of fish, he will pour upon you a rich harvest, in the morning he will rain bread cakes down on you, in the evening a torrent of wheat."

p. 182, *"I laid out the structure, I drafted plans:* This line actually occurs a dozen lines later; I have moved it forward.

p. 183, *rope makers brought their ropes, and children / carried the tar. The poor helped also, / however they could—some carried timber, / some hammered nails, some cut wood:* Literally, "[. . .] heavy axe. The young men were [. . .], the old men carried palm-fiber rope, the rich men carried pitch, the poor brought the [. . .] tackle."

p. 183, *an acre:* Literally, "1 *ikû*" = 3,600 m ^{2} = .89 acres.

p. 183, *two hundred feet:* Literally, "120 cubits" = 180 feet.

p. 183, *the ship's height was divided in seven:* "The boat as described is clearly a cube, not at all like ordinary Mesopotamian boats, and is probably a theological allusion to the dimensions of a ziggurat, the Mesopotamian stepped temple tower. The ziggurat was a massive solid structure with a square base and four to seven levels, the maximum height being the same as the length and width; it served as a monumental platform for a temple that stood on top" (Kovacs, p. 99). "The ship's . . . volume (about 7,600 tons) is condensed in the extreme . . . The Biblical account (Gen. 6) speaks of three storeys; the Ark measured 300 cubits in length, 50 cubits in breadth, and 30 cubits in height (about 20,000 tons)" (translated from Tournay and Shaffer, pp. 228–29).

p. 183, *three thousand gallons:* Literally, "3 *šár*," which, according to Bottéro, equals 10,800 l. (2,808 gal.).

p. 184, *I gave my palace:* Utnapishtim's generosity is, of course, pointless: if his faith in Ea's words is justified, both the gift and the gifted will soon be underwater.

p. 185, *No one could see through the rain, it fell / harder and harder, so thick that you couldn't / see your own hand before your eyes:* Literally, "One couldn't see another, people couldn't recognize one another in the downpour."

p. 186, *Anu's palace in the highest heaven:* "[The Mesopotamians] imagined at least three superposed celestial vaults: the highest was the dwelling of the sovereign and founder of the divine dynasty" (Bottéro, p. 191).

p. 186, *Aruru:* Literally, "the goddess." "It is customary to take ᵈ*ištar* as a proper noun. However, the following line, which develops the idea further, shows that the mother goddess is the subject here . . . Ištar is quite out of place as the lamenting goddess on this occasion. The parallel passage of OB Atram-ḫasīs has a similar couplet with *il-tum* in the first line and ᵈ*ma-mi* in the second . . . thus I take ᵈ*ištar* as a common noun, anticipating *bēlet-ilī* (. . . for another example in SB Gilgameš see SB I 274, where ᵈ*ištarī ummišu,* 'the goddess, his mother,' is Ninsun)" (George, *BGE,* II, p. 886).

p. 186, *when I spoke up for evil in the council of the gods!:* In the first passage about the gods' decision, p. 181, Aruru is not involved, and no mention is made of a council of the gods.

p. 186, *Their lips were parched, crusted with scabs:* "Not having human beings to provide them with offerings, they are dying of thirst and hunger. (Thus they later swoop down onto the final banquet)" (Bottéro, p. 192).

p. 187, *as flat as a roof:* "In this hot country, in which rain is quite rare, the roofs were, and still are, entirely flat, and serve as terraces" (Bottéro, p. 192).

p. 187, *a half mile away:* 14 x 10 *ninda* = 1,680 cubits = 2,520 feet.

p. 187, *For six days and seven nights, the mountain / would not release it:* Literally, "One day, a second day, Mount Nimush held the ship and would not release it. A third day, a fourth day, Mount Nimush held the ship and would not release it. A fifth day, a sixth day, Mount Nimush held the ship and would not release it."

p. 188, *her necklace of lapis lazuli:* "A necklace with carved lapis lazuli fly beads, representing the dead offspring of the mother goddess Belet-ili/Aruru" (Kovacs, p. 102).

p. 189, *how did it happen that you so recklessly / sent the Great Flood:* Here Ea, like Aruru a few lines above, seems to have forgotten that he and three other great gods collaborated in Enlil's decision. Perhaps Sîn-lēqi-unninni has used two different and conflicting traditions about Ea's involvement and Enlil's sole responsibility.

p. 190, *but be merciful, do not allow all men / to die because of the sins of some. / Instead of a flood, you should have sent / lions to decimate the human race, / or wolves, or a famine, or a deadly plague:* Literally, "Be lenient, lest he be destroyed; bear with him, lest [. . .]. Instead of sending the Flood, let a lion arise to diminish the human race. Instead of sending the Flood, let a wolf arise to diminish the human race. Instead of sending the Flood, let famine arise to destroy the land. Instead of sending the Flood, let pestilence arise to destroy the land."

p. 190, *I only whispered it to a fence / and Utnapishtim happened to hear:* Literally, "I made a dream appear to Atrahasis, and thus he heard the secret of the gods." "The poet betrays his source by calling his hero Atrahasis here [instead of Utnapishtim]" (Tournay and Shaffer, p. 239). "Ea defends himself against the charge that he broke the solemn oath not to speak to any human about the flood decided upon by Enlil: he did not 'speak' to Utnapishtim, since he only 'made a dream appear'; and if he did 'speak,' it was to 'his reed fence' and not to any human. Ea is the cleverest of the gods and, as such, is Jesuitical well *avant la lettre*" (Bottéro, p. 196). In *Atrahasis,* by contrast, he is completely straightforward: "Enki (=Ea) made his voice heard / And spoke to the great gods, / 'I did it, in defiance of you! / I made sure life was preserved' " (tr. Dalley).

p. 191, *at the source of the rivers:* In an earthly paradise reminiscent of Eden, which was at the source of four rivers (Genesis 2:10–14). "This distant place" has a Greek echo as well, in *Works and Days,* ll. 168 ff. (Hesiod is speaking of the fourth age, the age of heroes or demigods):

> But to other heroes Zeus gave a home and sent them
> far from all men, to the end of the earth. And there,
> untouched by sorrow, they live in the isles of the blessed
> along the shore of the fathomless, deep-swirling ocean,
> blissful heroes for whom the luxuriant earth
> three times a year bears fruit that is sweet as honey.

p. 191, *How would they know that you deserve it? / First pass this test: Just stay awake / for seven days. Prevail against sleep, / and perhaps you will prevail against death:* Literally, "Come, don't sleep for six days and seven nights."

p. 193, *Look down, friend, / count these loaves that my wife baked and put here / while you sat sleeping. This first one, rock-hard, / was baked seven days ago, this leathery one / was baked six days ago, and so on for all / the rest of the days you sat here sleeping. / Look. They are marked on the wall behind you:* Literally, "[Come,] Gilgamesh, count your loaves, and may [the days you slept] be made known to you. Your [first] loaf [is dried hard], the second is leathery, the third is soggy, the fourth has turned white, the fifth is spotted with mold, the sixth is fresh, the seventh was still baking on the coals when I touched you and you woke up."

p. 196, *If you find this plant:* "These instructions are clearly abbreviated, since they omit most of the information that Gilgamesh needed in order to act as he did" (Dalley, p. 134).

p. 196, *Gilgamesh dug a pit on the shore / that led down into the Great Deep:* "Gilgameš digs a shallow pit in the beach and soon reaches the water table. The fact that he makes the hole on land, not at sea, becomes clearer later, when he complains that he cannot rediscover it because the tide will have washed away any trace. The water table is the uppermost level of the cosmic domain of Ea, which in Ūta-napišti's realm is particularly accessible. Consequently the pit gives him immediate access to the subterranean Apsû. He dives down into the water, finds the plant but does not return the way he came. Instead he rises from the Apsû by way of the sea and, emerging just offshore from Ur-šanabi, is carried back to land by the surf" (George, *BGE*, I, pp. 523–24).

p. 197, *If that succeeds:* I have followed an alternative reading of George's, *šum-ma,* "if," rather than *šumšu,* "its (*or* his) name": "If the old man grows young (again), / I will eat some myself" (George, *BGE,* I, p. 723).

p. 197, *At four hundred miles they stopped to eat, / at a thousand miles they pitched their camp:* Literally, "At 20 *bēr* (= 216 kilometers, or about 134 miles) they stopped to eat, at 30 *bēr* (= 324 km., 201 mi.) they pitched their camp." Even though this is not explicitly a three-day march, the lines are a verbatim repetition of the march to the Cedar Forest, and I have kept the same distances.

p. 197, *it cast off its skin:* "This sudden sloughing is a symbol of immortality. The serpent was considered in the ancient Near East an animal of prolonged life, beneficent and healing, whence the emblem of the caduceus" (Tournay and Shaffer, p. 245).

p. 198, *a reptile:* Literally, "the lion of the ground," an epithet for the snake.

p. 198, *I plucked it from the depths, and how could I ever / manage to find that place again? / And our little boat—we left it on the shore:* Literally, "Now the tide has been rising for twenty leagues. When I opened the channel, I left the tools there: how could I find a landmark? I left the boat on the shore, and I have come too far to go back (*or,* in George's interpretation: Had I only turned away and left the boat on the shore!)."

BIBLIOGRAPHY

Bottéro, Jean, *L'Épopée de Gilgameš: Le grand homme qui ne voulait pas mourir,* Gallimard, 1992.

Dalley, Stephanie, *Myths from Mesopotamia: Creation, the Flood, Gilgamesh and Others,* Oxford University Press, 1989, revised edition 2000.

Ferry, David, *Gilgamesh: A New Rendering in English Verse,* Farrar, Straus and Giroux, 1992.

Foster, Benjamin R., *The Epic of Gilgamesh: A New Translation, Analogues, Criticism,* Norton, 2001.

Gardner, John, and John Maier, with the assistance of Richard A. Henshaw, *Gilgamesh: Translated from the Sîn-leqi-unninnī version,* Knopf, 1984.

George, A. R., *The Babylonian Gilgamesh Epic: Introduction, Critical Edition and Cuneiform Texts,* 2 vols., Oxford University Press, 2003.

George, Andrew, *The Epic of Gilgamesh: The Babylonian Epic Poem and Other Texts in Akkadian and Sumerian,* Penguin, 1999.

Kovacs, Maureen Gallery, *The Epic of Gilgamesh,* Stanford, 1989.

Sandars, N. K., *The Epic of Gilgamesh: An English Version with an Introduction,* Penguin, 1960, second revised edition 1972.

Schott, Albert, *Das Gilgamesch-Epos,* neu herausgegeben von Wolfram von Soden, 5th edition, Reclam, 1989.

Schrott, Raoul, *Gilgamesh: Epos*, Carl Hanser Verlag, 2001.

Speiser, E. A., in James B. Pritchard, *Ancient Near Eastern Texts Relating to the Old Testament*, third edition, Princeton University Press, 1969.

Tigay, Jeffrey H., *The Evolution of the Gilgamesh Epic*, University of Pennsylvania Press, 1982.

Tournay, Raymond Jacques, O.P., and Aaron Shaffer, *L'Épopée de Gilgamesh*, Les Éditions du Cerf, 1998.

GLOSSARY

ADAD God of the storm.

ANTU Anu's wife, mother of Ishtar (in one tradition).

ANU (Sumerian: An, "Sky") Son of the first pair of gods, Ansar and Kisar; god of the sky and father of the gods, specifically father of Enlil and Aruru.

ARURU ("Seed-loosener"; according to some scholars, the meaning of the name is unknown; also called Belet-ili, "Lady of the Gods") The mother goddess who created mankind with Ea's help. Sister (or wife) of Enlil; in some traditions, Anu's lover.

AYA Goddess of dawn, Shamash's bride.

BELET-SERI ("Lady of the Desert") Ereshkigal's scribe in the underworld, who holds the tablet recording life and death.

EA (Sumerian: Enki) The cleverest of the gods, god of intellect, creation, wisdom, magic, and medicine; son of Ansar and Kisar. He was also god of the freshwater subterranean ocean, *apsû,* the "Great Deep." He sent the Seven Sages to civilize mankind. Among other gifts, he created order in the cosmos, invented the plough, and filled the rivers with fish.

EANNA ("House of the Sky") The temple of Anu and Ishtar in Uruk.

ENKIDU (The name may mean "Lord of the Good Place" or, alternatively, "Enki's [=Ea's] creation," or "The Wild One.") A wild man made by gods, to be Gilgamesh's equal, in the Babylonian tradition (or, in the Sumerian tradition, to be his servant).

ENLIL (The name may mean "Lord of the Winds.") Son of Anu, father of Sîn, grandfather (in one tradition) of Shamash and Ishtar. With the help of Anu, Ea, and Aruru he governs the universe. He is sometimes friendly toward mankind, but can also be an irritable and capricious god who sends forth disasters such as the Great Flood. His cult center was at Nippur.

ENNUGI Sheriff or constable of the gods.

ERESHKIGAL ("Lady of the Great Earth") Ishtar's sister, queen of the underworld, which she rules with her consort, Nergal.

ETANA The thirteenth god-king of the Sumerian dynasty ruling the city of Kish (an ancient city-state of northern Babylonia), and the third king after the Flood. After his death he was a ruler in the underworld.

GILGAMESH (Sumerian: Bilgamesh; the Sumerian form of the name may mean "The Old Man Is a Young Man" or "The Ancestor Was a Hero.") A historical king of Uruk (ca. 2750 BCE; some scholars place him a century or so earlier). He was the fifth king of the First Dynasty of Uruk; according to legend, son of Lugalbanda and of the goddess Ninsun.

HUMBABA (Sumerian and Old Babylonian: Huwawa) The monstrous guardian of the Cedar Forest, appointed by Enlil to protect it by terrifying men away.

ISHTAR (Sumerian: Inanna, "Queen of Heaven") Patron deity of Uruk, goddess of sexual love and war; daughter of Anu, according to the tradition of Uruk; in other traditions, she is Anu's consort and daughter of Sîn.

LUGALBANDA ("Little Lord") King of Uruk, later deified. In one tradition he was the father of Gilgamesh, in another he was Uruk's guardian deity.

NAMTAR ("Decider of Fate") The minister or vizier of Ereshkigal and gatekeeper of the underworld.

NERGAL ("Lord of Erkalla") God of plague and war, later the husband of Ereshkigal.

NINSUN ("Lady of the Wild Cows") A minor Sumerian goddess known for her wisdom; Gilgamesh's mother.

NINURTA ("Lord of the Earth") Son of Enlil, chamberlain of the gods, god of agriculture, also honored as a war god.

NIPPUR Enlil's cult center, modern Nuffar, near 'Afaq in central Mesopotamia.

PUZUR-AMURRI ("Secret of the Western God") Utnapishtim's shipwright.

SHAMASH (Sumerian: Utu) The sun god, god of justice and patron of travelers and dream interpreters, and Gilgamesh's special protector. His cult centers were at Sippar and Larsa.

SHAMHAT (According to Bottéro, the name means "The Joyous One"; according to George, "something between 'Good-looking' and 'Well-endowed.' ") Priestess of Ishtar from Uruk, whose job was to civilize Enkidu.

SHIDURI (or Siduri; "She Is My Rampart"; some scholars says that the meaning is unknown.) Goddess of brewing and wisdom, who keeps a tavern at the edge of the world.

SHURUPPAK Utnaphistim's city in central southern Mesopotamia, between Nippur and Uruk. Modern Tell Fara.

SÎN (Sumerian: Nanna) The moon god, god of fertility, son of Enlil; according to some traditions, father of Shamash and Ishtar.

SÎN-LĒQI-UNNINNI ("Sîn Is the One Who Accepts a Prayer") The author/editor of the Standard Version of *Gilgamesh*. He lived sometime in the thirteenth to eleventh centuries BCE.

SUMUQAN (Sumerian: Shakkan) A god of the wilderness, the protector of wild animals.

TAMMUZ (Sumerian: Dumuzi, "Faithful Son") Lover and husband of Ishtar, sent by her to the underworld.

URSHANABI ("Servant of Two-Thirds"; Old Babylonian: Sursunabu) The boatman of Utnapishtim, who sails across the Waters of Death, which divide the garden of the gods from the paradise where Utnapishtim lives forever. ("Two-thirds" refers to Ea, whose symbolic numerical value was 40, two-thirds of Anu's 60.)

URUK An ancient city in southern Mesopotamia. Modern Warka.

UTNAPISHTIM ("He Who Found Life"; Sumerian: Ziusudra, "Life of Long Days") King of Shuruppak who survived the Great Flood and was made immortal. He is called Atrahasis ("Supremely Wise") in the poem of that name.

ACKNOWLEDGMENTS

I am deeply grateful to Michael Katz, my dear friend and agent, and to my excellent editor, Leslie Meredith. I am also grateful to Chana Bloch and John Tarrant for their many useful suggestions; to Benjamin R. Foster for generously pointing out some mistakes and misunderstandings on my part; to Martha Levin, Carissa Hays, Cassie Dendurent Nelson, Paul O'Halloran, and Phil Metcalf of Free Press for taking good care of the book; to Eric Fuentecilla, Joel Avirom, and Jason Snyder, the designers who made it so beautiful; and to Katie, for everything.

ABOUT THE AUTHOR

Stephen Mitchell's many books include the bestselling *Tao Te Ching*, *The Gospel According to Jesus*, *Bhagavad Gita*, *The Book of Job*, *Meetings with the Archangel*, *The Frog Prince*, *The Selected Poetry of Rainer Maria Rilke*, and *Loving What Is* (written with his wife, Byron Katie). His website is www.stephenmitchellbooks.com.